An Immortal Sorceress
PREQUEL

POWER OF THE SORCERESS

KRISTA WALSH

RAVEN'S QUILL PRESS

OTTAWA, ON

Power of the Sorceress / WALSH -- 1st ed.

Paperback ISBN: 978-1-998398-02-7

For the dancers, the lovers, and the fighters

1

Emrick

Palonia, Northern England - October 1147

T HE FINAL CORPSE crumbled to dust beneath my bare hand. After hours of labour, the evidence of the massacre that had happened last night was cleared. The remaining carnage—the blood-soaked grass, the neglected bonfires, the pervading silence—was out of my control. Time and the elements would handle everything else.

The sight of all these sorcerers meeting their gruesome, drawn-out end had left me tired, disgusted, and ready to disappear into the afterlife for a decade or so to try to rid myself of the memory.

Three hundred men, women, and children—the entire

population of this isolated sorcerer's village—killed in an act of brutal magic, a betrayal by three of their own.

Usually I escorted one or two souls at a time, people who had reached the end of their natural magical lifespan or succumbed to some accident. Rarely did I encounter illness among the supernatural, though it happened.

Events like this made me glad I no longer counted myself among humanity. After five hundred years serving Death, I was no more human than the wind that rippled the surface of the lake.

Last night had been the first time in over a century I'd surrounded myself with the laughing, breathing, dancing masses. Claiming to be a sorcerer from a southern village, I'd arrived at the beginning of the festival just as they lit their bonfires, drawn by a few previous deaths—rehearsals, it turned out—and whispers of something larger planned. I was curious to see if the two-faced sorceresses behind the attacks would succeed in their mission of binding a demon to gain immortality.

The result of the ritual had been nothing but blood and screams, and although a bright red light had spread across the ground where the traitors had stood, I hadn't seen any evidence of a demon. And considering I'd discovered no survivors as I performed my rounds and turned each empty body to dust, I suspected the immortality part had failed as well.

I couldn't have prevented the deaths of the innocent, no

matter how much I might have wished to after spending the evening with them. It was not my place to help people defy Death, only to escort them across that final barrier. To involve myself would mean sacrificing a fragment of my soul to the afterlife that bound me. Too many fragments lost would transform me into a shadow, a wraith, and while I often wondered if it would be kinder to myself to fade away—to lose my memories, any sense of who I was—I feared that emptiness the way mortals feared Death. Nothing was worth that change.

Not even the woman with the deep blue eyes and a clear laugh like a burbling brook who'd set fire to my blood in a way I hadn't experienced in hundreds of years. I'd been so tempted to warn her away. Instead, I'd held my tongue and appreciated her glow of life all the more knowing it was about to go out.

If I'd known what was to come, how the full brutal ritual would play out, maybe I would have accepted the consequences and warned her anyway. Though what kind of life would she have had as the sole survivor of her clan? Nothing but heartache and nightmares. She was better off as she was, at peace with the rest of them.

Now my task was complete. I was free to return to the afterlife and put this mess behind me. Free to leave the strange tug in my chest that had formed during the sorceresses' ritual. I rubbed the spot between my ribs where the tug seemed to originate, trying to dispel the odd sensation, but it didn't fade.

I felt the urge to walk forward, to follow the pull wherever it led me, but I ignored it. This life held nothing for me anymore.

I summoned the mist that would take me out of this world but stopped when a soft, broken voice called for me to wait.

I froze mid-stride. It wasn't possible that anyone should be here. This far north, hidden in the hills, the sorcerers' village was a secret few knew, and those who did were now mixed with the land that had been their home. The pull in my chest grew more intense, like an anchoring tether dragging me backwards. As much as I wanted to block out that voice, having nothing to offer some strange, wandering passerby, I couldn't do it.

I obeyed the drawing pressure and turned around—only for my breath to stutter on seeing a young woman standing in the empty field, her hair, skin, clothing slick with drying blood.

It shouldn't have been possible. I'd checked every corpse, moved one by one through the entire community of sorcerers that had perished here.

By the twigs clinging to her hair and the dirt pressed into her skin, I suspected she must have run before the ritual ended. Hidden in the woods. Waited until the silence confirmed the threat was over.

A breeze picked up and blew leaves and charred wood from the dying bonfires as we stared at each other. It caught the bottom of her skirt, but the blood had weighed it down so much the fabric barely shifted.

"You." Her eyes widened as she took in my face, and beneath the blood, she paled.

I gritted my teeth and prepared to curl my lip at her terrified accusations—a tool of Death, a spirit—but instead of fear, she lurched towards me on unsteady legs, stopping once she was close enough to look me in the eye.

"You've taken them. Take me, too. I beg you."

Her desperation washed over me, and a lump formed in my throat. I thought I'd grown immune to human emotion. Over the centuries, I'd been witness to so many tears, to so many people pleading for their loved ones to return to them, that I'd stopped feeling it on their behalf. Stopped registering it altogether.

But this woman…

I recognized her. I hadn't earlier with her features so covered in gore, but nothing could hide those striking blue eyes, as deep and dark as an ocean, lulling me into their current.

Gone was her sweet laugh and vivacious glow. Gone was the relaxed confidence she'd carried that first drew my eye. Gone was the woman who had so nearly made me break the one rule imposed on me by Death to never get involved.

I thought of her as she was last night. Her thick black hair loose down her back, her eyes sparkling, her smile bright. She'd stood with a younger version of herself—a sister, most likely—laughing over something she had said, and then a man had come up and handed her an infant boy who she'd tossed in the air and spun in circles until he screamed with laughter. She'd smothered his face in gentle kisses and leaned towards the man, who'd kissed her with such gentle passion my heart had clenched with jealousy.

She'd been so full of life.

Happy.

A hard contrast to this blood-soaked figure in front of me, surrounded by the loss of her entire kin. Alive by some strange, inexplicable turn of events.

Now she was asking me to send her after them, but it was out of my power to comply. "If you survived this tragedy, then it's not your time. Death does not accept those who are not due to receive it."

I wished I could say more, offer some form of comfort, give in to that tug urging me to help, but it made no sense for me to try. She and I were not the same. I was Death, and she had somehow clung to life.

I turned once more to the mist, but again she called to me, and again I felt the pull that brought me to a halt.

A sob caught in her throat as she staggered forward. "Please. You can't leave me here. This is all I've ever known. My son—these people—they're all I had. Everything is gone."

I turned back and stared into eyes growing wilder by the moment. She rubbed at her arms, then dropped them as she realized she was rubbing the blood of the fallen into her clothes. But as though her hands felt too empty, she gripped her skirts, squeezing so tightly her knuckles shone white through the red. At the sight of the madness sweeping over her expression as she faced the idea of being trapped here in the emptiness of her existence, the walls I'd formed to distance myself from humanity shattered. The sensation was cold, but beautiful in its novelty. It had been too long since I'd felt anything this poignant, and for a moment, I couldn't breathe.

Too late, reason and reality caught up to me. "I'm sorry—truly sorry—but I cannot help you."

I needed to escape before I succumbed to the heart-wrenching stare that had pierced my empty soul and brought to life a part of me I'd long believed had withered. My skin burned to be closer to her. I yearned to put my arms around her and hold her until she stopped trembling. Her beauty, her energy, the depth of her pain consumed me, and I feared if I stayed another moment, I would lose myself completely.

The mist wrapped around me, and I stepped into it, but before the doorway to the afterlife shut, she threw herself at me and latched on to my bare hand.

A gasp sucked through my teeth at the contact and the sparks that blasted through my flesh, my blood, my bone. I was filled with horror at what she'd done and shock that she'd caught me off guard. A deep throb reverberated in my heart where that tether had so suddenly come into existence.

Contact with my skin would jerk her body forward in time until she crumbled to dirt in an instant. Decomposed, returned to the earth like the rest of her family.

It's what should have happened.

Instead, her fingers wrapped around mine and tightened, her eyes so wide the blue shone through the splashes of blood, like the heart of fire through the flame.

The first living human contact I'd had in five hundred years, and it came from the woman whose closeness set me alight. The pulse in her wrist tapped against my hand, and every beat matched mine, quick and hard.

With each thump of her heart, the tether in my chest responded, and the truth of what had happened during the ritual became clear.

She hadn't run into the woods to escape the spell. She'd run to escape the devastation she alone had survived.

Those three sorceresses had set out to bind their souls to a demon. They had drained the blood of every member of their community to do it. As far as I had seen, their spell had failed. All three betrayers had fallen, and I hadn't seen them rise again.

As I stared at this broken woman, felt the tug of connection between us, I understood.

The ritual hadn't failed; it had ricocheted. Instead of summoning a demon, the spell had found me, a half-spirit already on this plane, standing too close to the tragedy being carried out around me. And somehow, for whatever reason, this sorceress had reaped the results. I wasn't the one tethered—she was, her life tied to mine. Bound to Death to live forever. A bizarre twist of fate that left me as stunned as she appeared to be.

Did she know what it meant that she was still standing?

Perhaps not yet, but she would in time. Gods knew she'd have plenty of it to work things out.

But she would have to do it on her own. She might make my soul sing, but she wasn't the first woman to have that effect on me. I'd made the mistake once of being drawn in, and the result had been eternal servitude. I wasn't about to accept the consequences of making yet another unbalanced deal.

"Please," she said. The single word in her quiet voice broke my fragile resolve, which I accepted had been nothing but posturing. She'd claimed my heart from the first, fool that I was.

It would break all the rules to take her with me—bring me a tiny step closer to the shadows that beckoned—but the bond between us wouldn't let me leave her.

I swallowed around the rock in my throat. "What's your name?" I barely recognized my own voice, as rough as it was with yearning and pain and no small amount of self-recrimination.

At first, she didn't seem able to answer as her lips wobbled and her eyes filled with tears. She calmed herself before they fell, a feat of such strength that I was swept even further under her spell. "Katerina."

Katerina. From the Greek word for pure. Someone from Palonia must have travelled far to come back with a name like that.

In this moment, she embodied the concept, and the disparity between us shook me like a lightning bolt. If she was purity, I was corruption, but despite the darkness I carried within me, I knew my purpose had shifted. I had no choice but to watch out for her. Indulging in this bond might chip away at my soul, but ignoring it would strip me of everything else.

"Very well, Katerina, come with me."

I pulled my hand from hers, unable to handle the continued thrill of her touch but longing for more the moment we broke contact.

She hesitated for a heartbeat before following, and the carnage of her whole world faded behind us.

2

Katerina

England - December 1147

I WOKE UP screaming again.

Every night, the same nightmares yanked me into wakefulness.

The same shrieks of despair as my people clawed at their skin to relieve their itching only to release more blood from their veins until the air was thick with it.

Grief wrapped around me in a choking miasma of pain and horror. But I pressed it down and tucked it as far as possible from my conscious mind to avoid being overwhelmed by it.

No matter how hard I wrestled, however, the scene pierced my thoughts and insisted on playing out behind my eyelids.

In actuality, I hadn't been near my family when it had happened, having left the festival before the ritual began to find help for my ailing son. But in dreams… in dreams I held Rowan in my arms, heard his wailing—*don't think of it. Don't think of it*—and stood next to my husband. My sister. My parents. My grandmother. All the people who mattered to me, screaming in agony before they collapsed.

Trapped in my mind, I choked on the thick, metallic scent as the airborne blood sank into my pores, trickled down the back of my throat, encased me. Turned me into whatever I was now.

So many times in the past few months I'd scrubbed my skin raw to rid myself of the sticky, putrid feel of it, but still it lingered.

Awake, I was able to suppress my emotions, wrap myself in numbness, knowing if I allowed myself to feel any of it, I would be forced to feel *all* of it. And if that happened, my strained sanity would snap. But I had no control in my sleep, and every night I drifted closer to madness.

There was no escape. Not for me. My family had suffered— intensely, brutally—but their suffering was over, while mine continued, night after night and day after day. I was haunted every waking moment by what I'd seen. What I'd heard. Smelled. Tasted.

I retched into the grass next to where I lay, and when I

looked up, I spotted a pair of silver eyes framed by long lashes gleaming in the reflection of the low-burning fire. Strands of the man's blond hair, tied back by its usual leather strap, had fallen loose, highlighting the trim golden beard along his strong jawline. He wore his white shirt unlaced at the neck, the sleeves tucked into thick leather gloves, the bottom tucked into a pair of black breeches. He wore no cloak to fend off the cold, but I doubted he felt the scrape of winter's touch.

Gàst-iadman. Spirit-herder.

A servant of Death, tasked with escorting the dead across the barrier between this life and the next.

After leading me away from my ravaged village, he'd introduced himself as Emrick and proceeded to tell me that Alodie, Mae, and Blythe's ritual had bound me to him, leaving me immune to time, immune to Death.

Something I struggled to accept.

He had rarely left my side since then, and although he didn't often speak and made certain to keep his distance, I was grateful for his steadying presence. The solitude in these empty stretches of land left me far too alone with my thoughts. Without him close, whatever strings of sanity remained to me would have snapped weeks ago.

"More dreams?" he asked, his voice low, gruff.

He never slept. Not that I'd seen, anyway. But of course not—why would he? He wasn't human.

I nodded as I sat up and arranged my cloak over my knees to keep myself warm. The material was new and scratchy, not my worn-in cloak that was folded at the end of my bed, so far away from where I now slept. I'd never gone back to the cottage where I'd lived with my family—back to see the empty cradle where Rowan slept, the bed where Shep and I had spent our nights. There was nothing there I'd wanted badly enough to suffer that torture.

Everything I wore now came from Emrick. Gifts from him whenever he left me only to return some time later in his swirl of mist. Just like his presence, I appreciated the warm, heavy woollen clothes against the harsh winter temperatures, but the unfamiliarity of the cloth was more salt in the wound of my grief.

"I was thinking we might head west," he said. "There's another sorcerer's village not far from here. Another week, maybe. You'll find support there. People who can help you."

The idea of surrounding myself with my own kind stopped my breath. My pulse leapt, and my hands went cold. A few short words from him, and the ground disappeared beneath me. Having to explain what had happened to my community when I hadn't opened my mouth to speak in three months? Having to explain how they'd died?

How I'd survived?

Me, the failed sorceress who hadn't even tried to use her

magic to take the traitors down?

They would flay the coiled dragon tattoo, the mark of my sorcerer's clan, off my thigh. And they would be right to do so. I was useless—the least deserving of my village to find myself suddenly immortal.

I wondered if Emrick thought the same. Likely, he was eager to drop me off in the nearest village and continue on his way without me. He hadn't asked for me to be bound to him. He never showed any resentment, but I didn't doubt it was there, which only made me feel smaller.

I wished I could shrink more. Shrink until I snapped out of existence.

I wanted to throw myself at him and beg him not to take me there, not to put me through that hell, but the words—like all words—caught in my throat. Tears spilled down my cheeks as I pulled my knees to my chest and wrapped my arms around them.

"It was just an idea," Emrick said softly. "I thought you might have gotten tired of wandering the woods, staying away from everyone."

He was wrong. It was exactly what I wanted. People terrified me. The few villages we'd neared, the sounds and smells, had overwhelmed me with the intensity of *life* running through the narrow streets. The accents, so like my own, kept turning my head as I expected to see someone I knew running up the lane towards me—but they never would again.

They were gone, and I was alone. Alone except for the *gàst-ladman*, who probably wanted to leave me behind.

I forced myself to breathe through the panic that squeezed my heart and drained the blood from my face.

"If you prefer, we'll keep walking," he said. "You can let me know when you're ready to head somewhere specific."

He held my gaze, and in his stare, I saw none of the impatience I thought to find. Gradually, my breathing slowed, and I nodded again.

Emrick pursed his lips in acknowledgement and turned his attention back to the fire. "Try to get a few more hours' sleep. Dawn's a long way off yet."

More months passed, and still my skin didn't fit comfortably around this new life.

On the contrary, the farther we journeyed into a world I'd never stepped foot in, the more of a stranger I felt—to the people we passed, to the earth beneath my feet, to the voices in my ear, and to myself.

My vivid nightmares refused to let me sleep. I woke up feeling my son's weight in my arms only to find him not there, and the emptiness was beyond my ability to cope. I lost the will to eat. Loud noises made me jump, and the only comfort I had was the hum of a bond around my heart that neither party involved had asked for.

One day, after once again trying to scrub the sticky sensation of my family's blood from my flesh, I tried lying face-down in a shallow river, waiting for my lungs to fill and my heart to give out, thinking only of Rowan and the others who'd left before me.

I woke up hours later, still breathing, next to a roaring fire and covered in wolf pelts, with barely an ache in my chest to show for my efforts. Emrick wasn't there, but I knew he'd been the one to drag me out of the river. Had he rescued me or simply taken me away from a failed attempt to leave this unwanted plane?

After that, I stopped eating or drinking for the span of weeks, suffering the aches and pains in my muscles as they spasmed and weakened but always healed until, finally, Emrick had coaxed me into swallowing a bite of bread. I'd given in, knowing my efforts to waste away were futile.

Death didn't want me.

As the full breadth of that truth sank in, the future weighed on me even heavier. I had no way out, no purpose, nowhere to go.

The feeling was made worse when Emrick started leaving more often. Never without warning and always with a promise to return, but I found myself alone for days at a time while he carried out his task of escorting the magical dead to the afterlife.

I didn't travel far when he was gone. Not because I didn't think he'd be able to find me, but because with no destination in mind, with my only goal being to keep Palonia at my back, I didn't see the point. Yet even so, it was strange to be by myself for the first time in my life. The large world bore down on me, every tree, rock, and blade of grass taunting me.

Shep had been a great hunter, both of magical beasts and mundane. He'd led many missions to eliminate the creatures that stalked the hills outside Palonia and threatened to reveal our kind to the mundane communities. I doubted I could fend off a squirrel.

Keeping our secret was one of the greatest purposes of our village, along with passing down the skills and knowledge of our magic to ensure it wasn't lost. Already our sorcerer powers were on the wane, our blood thinning as our hunters died, our weaker sorcerers left the village and married mundanes, or, like me, couldn't damn well learn their magic.

I summoned a flame over my fingers and set alight the tinder and sticks I'd piled, building a small fire as night came on. With effort, I drew on my power until the fire spread and covered my palm and the backs of my fingers. It licked over my runed gloves, my only souvenir of a life lost, tickled my fingers that were bare from the knuckles down, and tripped over the leather that stretched up to my elbow.

And there it stopped.

There it had always stopped.

My mother had been able to create ice sculptures so lifelike they'd made the children shriek with terrified delight. My father had summoned lightning bolts that rivalled those that struck the earth during the strongest storms. My primary instructor, Alodie, could wield fire in a way that put nature to shame.

I'd grown up surrounded by so much magic, being told I would one day be capable of just as much… and all I could do was wrap my arms in flames.

Or ice.

In a blink, the fire disappeared, absorbing into my skin as I drew in the heat to rapidly cool the air around me. Vines of frost replaced it, decorating my hands in delicate sworls of glittering lace, flaunting its intricate beauty as though it weren't my greatest shame.

Because while I had never learned to project my magic outwards, I knew how to draw it inwards, something no one else in my village could do. Something no one had bothered to learn because how would it ever be useful?

But wasn't that how I'd saved my own skin while everyone else collapsed to the ground during the ritual?

I'd suffered the same gnawing, burning, raging itch as they

had. I'd torn open welts on my arms and neck, spilling my blood so it joined the droplets in the air.

In my panic, I'd summoned my ice. Covered myself in it as I'd dropped to the ground and clawed my fingers into the dirt.

I hadn't tried to stop the women chanting around the steaming pot.

I hadn't tried to run to my family to get them to stop scratching.

I'd hunkered down under my beautiful, protective shield, squeezed my eyes shut, and waited for it to be over.

My reward was immortality and loneliness.

I hated myself.

I hated my weakness.

And now I was trapped with both for eternity. My baby boy torn from me, my husband dead, the rest of my family gone.

The grief I'd pushed back for three months ripped through the walls I'd built around my heart, squeezed my soul, and spilled like burning oil through my blood.

Alone with my agony, I voluntarily broke my silence for the first time in months and filled the dark forest with my screams.

3

Emrick

England - April 1150

Katerina's blue eyes followed me as I passed through the monotonous grey of the afterlife.

There was nowhere I could go to escape their tide, yet whenever I came too close, I felt myself sliding closer to drowning in them.

In the afterlife, the plane I'd called home for the past half-millennium, little surrounded me except vague shapes through the fog. Beyond that misty veil lay a different world from that of the living, one leached of colour and brilliance. Empty trees, stretches of barren field, a drab, limitless sky. Beautiful for everything it represented—the offset of what had come before—but a beauty I'd only begun to appreciate decades after I'd accepted my place within it.

Now that beauty had been overshadowed, and I'd spent less time here over the past three years, constantly drawn back to the world I'd sworn I'd put behind me. My place was no longer among the living. I no longer had cause nor the right to walk alongside the woman whose existence stirred the empty spaces of my heart, yet try as I might, I couldn't keep away from her.

Every time I stepped through the mist, bringing her gifts in the form of basic necessities, her expression brightened, and the sight of it filled me with such a mix of relief and pain that I didn't know which was strongest.

We walked without speaking, without direction. She needed to put distance between her and the home she'd lost but resisted going anywhere that might take her in. We kept to the woods, skirting villages, as aimless as we'd been from the beginning.

Nightmares I wished I could battle away tormented her. Night after night for three years, she woke up screaming, covered in sweat, fighting the monsters that followed her no matter how far we moved from Palonia.

Even now, as she slept on the hard ground, the cool light of dawn spilling over the horizon to brush her pale skin and highlight the bruises of exhaustion under her eyes, her brow was furrowed and her shoulders were tense. Whimpers of fear spilled from her lips, and she clung to the folds of her cloak so tightly I was certain her fingernails would poke holes through it.

I wanted to wake her. Cradle her against my chest. Soothe her with gentle words and reassuring caresses until she calmed down and recognized the brightness of the morning.

But it wasn't my place.

For months after I'd led her away from the slaughter, I'd tried to resent the bond that tied us together. I hadn't wanted it, hadn't asked for it, was uncomfortable with the pulse of life in a heart that had been still for five hundred years.

More than anything, I wanted to resent the further loss of control over my soul, first indebted to Death and now caught up in the immortality of this sorceress. I felt as though my fate was no longer my own but split between these two powerful, external forces.

But I couldn't hold it against Katerina.

I found I couldn't even hold it against the women who'd bound us.

More than once, I played with the idea of finding a sorcerer who could break the bond and release us, but every time the suggestion reached my tongue, it died away. Not only because my experience as a sorcerer told me such a ritual would involve more blood, but also because the thought of breaking the tie that had revived me in such unexpected ways created an ache so deep it left me weak.

I'd gone from wanting nothing to do with this woman of the dragon clan to not being able to imagine a life without her.

My cracked and fragile dragon, unable to fly or breathe fire. On some days barely able to stand.

The smallest sounds frightened her. Every new place, new sight, new experience made her crowd me, as though I were the only shelter she trusted not to crush her.

The feeling honoured me. Humbled me. Terrified me. I had severed my ties to this world. After handing over my future in a doomed trade, I wanted nothing more than to keep my head down and stay focused. Allow the years to pass until I no longer noticed the rush of time and Death finally considered my debt served.

Until Katerina.

A realization that scared me more than anything else.

This sorceress had, through no fault of her own, cheated Death of the balance it so carefully preserved, and I was caught between them, consumed by the fire of one, owned by the other, wondering where I existed.

And, to a point, not caring as long as it meant saving this woman from herself.

It would be wiser of me to think of nothing except carrying out my responsibilities, serving solely as the guide to the afterlife instead of the worldly shepherd I'd become— ironic considering the wolf tattooed on my chest, a relic of my former sorcerer's clan—but I accepted that I'd left wisdom behind me.

I'd had no choice in this bond, and that rankled me. But I couldn't ignore the coincidence that the person on the other end of the tether was the first woman who'd caught my attention in five hundred years.

It made me think the Fates had more to do with my being in Palonia that night than any rumour of traitorous women.

Katerina could turn those piercing blue eyes on me and, with a single look, bring me to my knees and make me obey her every wish.

It was a dangerous game—one Death would not approve of if I didn't hold up my end of our deal. My only option was to play it safe. Keep my emotions to myself, never let on that she had such power over me, and pray I found my wits before I lost my way.

4

Katerina

England - February 1153

How long had I followed Death through the English forests?

It must have been close to six years, though I'd stopped counting the days long ago. Despite the passage of time, my grief ensnared me like a mantle I couldn't shake. I still hadn't uttered a word since I'd left Palonia, still battled the nightmares that haunted me almost every night.

The only constant was Emrick, and he'd left a few nights ago, leaving me alone to drag my feet through the snow.

Alone to face the pack of wolves that had closed in around me. Half a dozen slavering beasts starving after a lean winter, staring at little lone me as though I were a decadent feast.

I doubted they would be filled even if they devoured me down to the marrow. After so many years with no need and not much desire to eat, I was little more than five feet, four inches of skin and bone—barely a snack, let alone a threat.

Two of the beasts stepped forward, and I moved back, keeping my attention firmly on them. The moment I turned around, they'd attack. I told myself I didn't care—that perhaps being eaten would finally remove me from this world without connection or purpose or the will to keep breathing—but instinct took over where drive failed.

Digging deep into whatever strength I had after years of not exerting any, I tapped into my buried magic. It woke slowly in my centre, rolling like sludge through my core, over my arms, weighing me down, making my movements slow and sluggish. I raised my trembling hands, and fire coiled between my fingertips. It lapped at my gloves, which showed no sign of time's wear and tear, the leather imbued with magic just as the etched runes helped channel my power.

When the first wolf leapt, I was ready with a palm full of flame. I slapped the beast across the face, and it yelped as fire singed its muzzle. The others took it as a signal for them to join in, and before I could pump more fire into my hands, a set of jaws closed on my shoulder. Another set of sharp teeth locked on my leg and jerked me to the frozen earth.

The breath burst from my lungs at the impact, and I gasped to refill them, but the pain of torn flesh and muscle made it impossible for me to focus on the basic concept of inhaling. A suffocated scream choked me instead, forming a thick lump in my gut that prevented either air or sound from escaping.

My heart raced as my survival instinct kicked in, and I channelled more fire into my hands. It shot through my pores like tiny glowing embers that landed in the wolves' fur and caught. They growled and snarled at the irritation, but the flames weren't strong enough to spread, petering out as soon as the beasts hit the snow.

My frustration mixed with terror as my best attempts proved fruitless. I grasped for more magic, hating that my power was so weak. I came from greatness, had been intended for greatness, and was now left to appreciate how lacking I was.

Grief, rage, and despair spilled through me, each one fighting to overwhelm me.

The rage won.

I finally managed to suck in a breath and used it to centre my scattered thoughts as the wolves made their second assault. I flailed my limbs, refusing to be the easy target they thought me to be. The heel of my leather boot caught one wolf in the muzzle and sent him scurrying back. Another appeared in its place, and more searing pain cut through my thigh. Claws sliced into my back.

My screams came free and easy now, spilling through the trees, getting lost among the snow drifts. There was no one to hear me except the wolves, but I couldn't hold them back. My magic wasn't enough to fight them off—*I* wasn't enough.

Could they kill me? Was one well-aimed snap of those gaping jaws enough to push Death to pay attention? Or would some part of my consciousness remain in the belly of the beast? Would this unwanted immortality allow me to heal from being torn apart? Would I have to endure the agony as the scattered pieces of my ravaged flesh knitted back together?

Another set of teeth sank into my hip, and I knew I did not want to watch my body repair itself. More than that, I realized I didn't want to die.

A revelation, if a poorly timed one, after six years of dragging myself through this world, stuck at the age I was when time stopped.

My weak and limited magic had meant I'd been excluded from most of the physical training my village had put its sorcerers through, leaving me woefully unprepared for this fight, but I refused to give up.

I clenched my fists and pulled my magic through my veins until it slipped past my fingers and skipped across the fur of the wolf that had launched at my arm. Smoke and fire filled the empty valley, and with howls of fear and pain, it bolted into the woods, a flaming beacon of my laughable power.

The other five wolves closed in, but this time I was ready with claws of my own in the form of flames licking from the tips of my fingers. When they drew close enough, I set my hands on two more wolves. Their fur caught, the flames spreading, engulfing them. They leapt away from me and tore wildly through the snow to escape the threat that followed them.

The other three moved warily now, and I hauled myself to my feet. Bright red blood stained the white snow in a circle around me—drips and spray and smears—but I didn't let myself look too closely in case I lost whatever focus I'd mustered.

One wolf took a tentative step towards me, then wisely turned and fled, snapping at the heels of a second wolf to herd it along beside it.

That left one. The skinniest among them. The most desperate. I doubted it had more than a few days left if it didn't eat something more substantial than its packmates' leftovers.

My vision wavered, and I stumbled where I stood, my legs losing the power to keep me upright. The wolf and I were in a similar state, and I couldn't help but pity it even as I grew more determined not to give in without a fight.

Though the fight was rapidly leaving me. If this creature showed a bit of patience, it wouldn't need to worry about losing its dinner. Already the heat of my magic had ebbed, curling deeper into my centre to keep my vitals warm as more of my blood painted the fresh snowfall.

I dropped to my knees. The wolf hunkered lower and bared its teeth, its hollowed flanks expanding and retracting with every hungry breath.

Black spots blocked my view, and I collapsed to my side. The part of me that remained rational struggled to summon my magic, but it drifted further out of reach with every slowing heartbeat.

I felt the itch of flesh working to pull itself together, my heart chugging to replace the blood I'd lost, but for now I didn't have the strength to move my fingers and pull my cloak over my shivering body. Anger pulsed through me that at the moment I'd chosen to live, I might be about to die, but not even my fury could renew my energy fast enough.

The wolf launched at me with a snarl, but before it struck, the air shimmered and paled in a sudden mist, and an arm reached out of the nothingness. A bare hand closed around the wolf's throat, and between blinks, the creature was gone, a pile of blackened dirt on the white ground.

The arm remained, covered in a white shirt that hugged a muscular bicep and a wide shoulder. A broad chest appeared next, followed by the rest of Emrick as he emerged from the afterlife. His hide breeches hugged his hips, his muscular thighs.

Even in my woozy state, he was the type of man to draw attention. Hadn't he captivated my sister on that fateful night six years ago? I remembered the way she and her friends had giggled and fawned, each of them trying to edge the other out of the way to catch his eye, and all of them failing.

Of course they had. He hadn't been there to flirt or play. He'd been there to carry out his duty. To guide the spirits of the dead to the afterlife.

I often felt like a stray dog following in his wake, desperate and pathetic, begging for the smallest scrap of kindness or connection. After so many years wandering forests, keeping away from people to avoid having to give an account of myself, I forgot what human contact felt like, but thanks to Emrick, I maintained my humanity. A small blessing, but one I couldn't overlook.

When he did leave me, the reasons for which he never gave but I assumed had to do with his responsibilities to Death, he always returned with food and clean clothing, and today was no exception. Something I was more than a little thankful for given my torn and bloodied state.

At the sight of me lying in the snow, dark clouds swept over his silver eyes. He released his hold on the bundle he carried and dropped to his knee by my side. I couldn't read his expression, as closed-off as it was, but my breath hitched in my chest when he reached for my face, hesitated, then brushed the hair out of my eyes. He was so careful not to come in contact with my skin, even with his glove on. At his closeness, I stayed statue-still, my breath growing quick and shallow, and wondered at the way his long fingers lingered so close to my cheek before he pulled them back.

"Are you all right?"

A quick inventory assured me all my wounds were on the mend, so I nodded. Though my body betrayed me as I attempted to rise to my feet, my legs shaking badly with the rush of the attack and the exertion of healing such severe injuries so quickly.

Emrick made no offer to help me, but I wouldn't have known how to react if he had.

He pulled on his other glove, then handed me the bundle of clothes. I hugged them to my chest and, breathing in the smell of him—campfire and loam—lingering in the wool, summoned my courage to take another step forward.

Realizing I wanted to live had been the first one, but the wolves had made it clear that to do so I would need to prepare myself for this world. I needed to be stronger, faster.

And I needed help to do it.

In all these years, I'd never asked Emrick for anything beyond leading me somewhere away from home, through a quiet country and a larger world I'd never explored.

That changed tonight.

As he turned to walk away, to lead me in our never-ending wander to nowhere, I said, "You were one of us once. A sorcerer."

My voice was rough from disuse, but it was enough to bring Emrick to a sharp stop. He turned to face me, his expression blank.

I knew it was true. Once and only once, I'd seen the twisted lines of the wolf tattooed on the left side of his chest. It was too similar a design to the dragon on my right thigh to be a coincidence. One of the southern sorcerer communities, if I remembered my studies correctly.

He stared at me with those eyes that reminded me of the moon rising overhead. "I was."

"Will you teach me?"

Confusion crossed his handsome features. "Teach you what?"

"How to use my magic."

He couldn't know how much it shamed me to ask. How embarrassing it was that after twenty-four years with my family, with the most experienced members of Palonia doing their best to show me the way, I had never mastered the abilities I'd been born with. A shadow of a sorceress compared to my peers.

His mouth twisted in an expression I couldn't read but at least didn't appear to be mockery. "I'm sorry, but I can't help you. Not like that. I should go."

He turned away, the air in front of him thickening as he prepared to leave me again.

"Please," I said, and the scene reminded me too much of

Palonia, how I'd begged him to take me away from the empty village. "If I'm to be stuck in the world for the rest of eternity, I need to be able to defend myself against wolves or whatever else I might come across. I'm helpless on my own."

He hesitated, one foot in the afterlife, the other firmly in the present. There was something in the way he looked at me that made me feel as though I'd bared more than my soul to him just now, and my cheeks flushed with heat.

"You no longer wish to be rid of me?" he asked. "Of your immortality, I mean?"

His curiosity was impossible to miss, but there was something else beneath it. I might have called it hope if I hadn't forgotten what it looked like.

"I don't," I said, hugging the bundle closer. "But if I'm to accept my fate, I can't be dependent on you to keep me safe. Please, will you teach me?"

"No," he said again, but this time there was a hint of apology in the refusal. Or maybe regret? "Not your magic. But…" He hesitated, looked into the mist as though he were arguing with himself. Finally, he bowed his head and drew a blade from a sheath around his thigh. "Let's see where we can get you with this."

The mist faded as he handed me the knife. It wasn't enough, not nearly, but it was one more step away from the life I'd known into whatever was to come.

5

Emrick

England - September 1157

FOR THE NEXT four years, I cursed myself for not walking away from Katerina's request.

Not only because of the sliver of myself I gave up to Death by agreeing to help her, but because of the time I now spent with her, no longer silently leading her through the empty countryside but actively working with her to ensure her safety.

Teaching her magic would have been out of the question. It would be far too intimate a practice between us, and far too big a change to the mortal world for Death to ignore.

Over the years, she asked twice more, and each time I refused, pleading ignorance. Which wasn't wholly untrue. It had been centuries since I'd traded power over the elements for manipulation of life itself, and I'd forgotten much of what I once knew.

Even the small offering of teaching her the basics with my knife meant closer proximity. More contact. I avoided as much as I could, escaping into the afterlife as often as possible, yet day after day, I was pulled back to her side by the bond and by my undeniable desire to be near her.

Which only grew now that she was speaking, asking me questions about myself and the world. The personal questions I put off as best I could, offering short answers that discouraged more questions. For the most part, she took the hint, though that didn't stop her from asking something else at the next opportunity.

Her questions about the world, however, I answered at length, captivated by the curiosity and interest that lit up her ocean eyes and not unaware that, soon enough, she would need to know more than I could tell her.

The world was changing, the mundane spreading while magic grew dimmer. Soon, I suspected, she would have no more woods to hide in. She would need to step back into civilization, where magic would have no place.

Where she would constantly struggle to find a place of her own.

"Why are you looking at me like that?" she asked, and I

pulled myself out of my thoughts, not aware I'd been looking at her at all.

She sat in the doorway of the alehouse barn where we'd stopped for the night. Her knees were pulled up to her chest, her skirt pulled down so it tucked under her toes. Moonlight fell through the trees to bathe her pale skin, and in this moment, she looked to be the goddess of the moon herself, gracing the mortal world with her presence.

I cleared my throat and picked at a loose piece of straw. "I was thinking about where we should go. We've run out of places in England to wander without turning around and returning north."

She leaned her head back against the wood, exposing the smooth skin of her throat. I licked my lips and averted my gaze.

"Shep used to tell me stories of other countries, but I always wondered if he made them up to entertain me. Now you tell me such wondrous things that I'm almost convinced."

The mention of her husband caused something in me to shift—a growling jealousy over the man she had loved. But I reminded myself that even if Shep weren't dead, there was no way I could take his place. Not given what I was.

"Everything I've said pales to the reality."

"I might like to see them."

She spoke to the moon, and I couldn't take my eyes off her, imagining what it would be like to show her my favourite secrets scattered across the globe.

I could take her through the mists wherever she wished to go… but somehow I knew such a jump would be too jarring. She was only just coming out of the shell she'd hidden in for ten years—I didn't want to move too quickly and send her scurrying back into it.

"We could start with France. Take a ship from Dover to Calais and make our way south."

"South is good." She rolled her head towards me, and my breath caught as I fell once more into the current of her eyes, almost black in the dim light. "Can I ask you a question?"

"You can, but I won't change my mind about teaching you magic."

The corner of her lip curled upwards, the expression the closest I'd seen her come to a smile since the night of the festival, and even that was rare. A treat for me whenever I earned it.

"How did you come to be what you are?"

"So handsome and charming?"

"Are you? I hadn't noticed."

I chuckled and dropped my gaze, savouring the moment, once again putting off answering her question. It wasn't a subject I enjoyed dwelling on. For all her curiosity, she'd shown remarkable restraint in asking about my history. Maybe it was the moonlight or the sense of peace drifting through the autumn-scented air that pushed her to ask tonight.

Finally, after the silence had stretched out long enough without either of us changing the subject, I said, "I made a deal."

"Did you get what you wanted out of it?"

A painful lump throbbed in my chest. "No."

"I'm sorry."

I looked up and found her attention once more focused outside. Had she lost interest already? I both hoped and feared that was the case.

"Would you make the deal again if you knew?"

Her second question caught me off guard, and I leaned back against the pile of hay pushed against the wall.

A hundred years ago, fifty, I would have said no. "Yes, I think I would."

She turned to face me, and there were so many things I wanted to say and so many reasons I would never say them. I found myself frozen, awaiting her next question.

It never came. She offered me that same small smile and returned her attention outside, as though she saw the pain written on my face and chose to be merciful. My heart beat a little harder, and I knew I had to leave before I did or said something I regretted.

"Good night, Katerina."

"Good night, Emrick."

I left her there, my secrets still my own.

6

Katerina

France - October 1197

AMAZING HOW FORTY years can feel like both an eternity and the blink of an eye.

If anyone had asked me what I'd done with those years, I don't know how I would have answered.

True to his word, when Emrick returned, we shifted our direction towards Dover.

I did my best to engage with people when we reached civilization, picking up local news, scrubbing the dirt from social habits that had gone grimy with disuse. Styles had changed, and I found myself rushing to keep up with them, picking up the shifts in language over time and learning the culture of every new society.

Emrick stayed with me as often as he could, offering insight and advice with every interaction, giving me history lessons with every new destination. He also continued teaching me to use his knife, and after so many decades, I no longer felt helpless, a relief now that we spent so much time among crowds.

The boat from Dover to Calais had me retching over the side for most of the trip, but the sights and sounds of the port when we arrived left me speechless. There were so many people speaking so many languages and wearing such different styles of clothing that my head spun with the effort of keeping track.

Despite my awe and fascination, the current of grief kept dragging me down into the murk. Every time I caught myself smiling or relaxing in the magic of our travels, guilt that I was here to enjoy it while the rest of my community was not hooked its claws into my mind.

As the fiftieth anniversary of the ritual arrived, I was again overwhelmed with the memory of my people's blood on my skin. Unable to bear it, I stripped down to nothing and stepped into the water in a cove tucked along the coast. I'd scrubbed myself raw so many times over the years I was amazed I had any skin left, but the heavy, greasy, sticky sensation remained.

The rough sand I scooped from the beach soon had my skin red and screaming. The water was cold despite the summer sun, but I wished it were colder. Cold enough to numb my outsides to match my insides.

A cool wind tickled the back of my neck, and a tendril of mist drifted over my shoulder. Shame weighed me down, and I curled in on myself to hide the bleeding scratches across my arms and stomach. At the sharp intake of Emrick's breath, I guessed my back revealed enough.

"Ah, Katerina, what have you done to yourself?" His voice was soft, concerned.

I heard a rustle of cloth as he set something down, but I didn't turn around, not wanting to see the look in his eyes. Although I heard no judgement or disappointment, I couldn't help but worry I'd find them.

"It's still there," I said when the silence stretched out long enough and he didn't move. "It doesn't matter how much I scrub or how often I wash, I still feel their blood on me, seeping into my pores." A shudder ran through me, and I wrapped my arms around my bare chest to ease the tremors. The sand spilled from my hands, and I pulled up my knees to hide more of myself.

The silence behind me persisted until, finally, Emrick stepped closer. When he spoke again, his voice came from lower down, right behind me. "You have nothing to feel guilty about. You did nothing wrong."

"I did." I turned at the waist to face him. He met my gaze, the liquid silver of his eyes filled with pain on my behalf, which only made me feel worse. "Do you know what I did when I realized what was happening? I covered myself in frost and froze my blood in place. That's how I survived. Because a strange quirk in my magic allowed me to defend myself when no one else in the village could do the same. And what did I do with that advantage? I stayed right where I was. I could have stopped them. I could have released my magic and died with the others. Instead, I knelt on the ground and cowered there while everyone else—from the oldest teachers to the youngest babe—*my babe*—"

I choked on my words and bowed my head as tears spilled down my cheeks.

It had been fifty years, and I'd never spoken of that night with Emrick. I'd never been able to put words to my cowardice, the survival instinct that had put my own life before my child's.

The community had always seen me as a failure because of my inability to master my magic, and that night I'd proved it to them one last time.

I scrubbed my tears away with the heel of my palm and turned my back on Emrick, wrapping my arms around my knees.

I waited for him to argue with me or offer comfort and readied myself to throw his words back in his face, but instead, after a while, he said, "You asked me once about the deal I made for my immortality."

The change in subject surprised me, and I turned again, this time shifting onto my knees to face him. The water kept me covered, but it wouldn't have mattered. His attention was on a rock he'd picked up and was now spinning between his fingers.

"You said you didn't get what you wanted out of the deal." I hadn't pressed at the time, understanding his need to keep his secrets, but I longed to know more about this strange half-spirit I followed.

He sucked on his teeth, as though debating if he could continue, but at last he shrugged. "When I made that deal, I was in love with the most incredible woman. Gabrielle. Gaby. She was strong, clever, loved to laugh. We'd been married five years, and I was the happiest man in the world. We were never blessed with children, but even so, I had her. And then she got sick." He shifted where he sat, dropped the rock, brushed the dirt off his hands, but still he didn't look at me, his gaze now resting on the trees over my head. "I summoned Death. Pleaded to trade her life for mine. Death offered me a deal—in exchange for my service when my time was over, she would be healed to live out her natural lifespan."

Shock lodged my breath in my throat. An eternity of servitude in exchange for a handful of decades? It hardly seemed like a fair trade.

"I didn't care what I was giving up," he said. "All that

mattered was that she would be well. So I agreed." He cupped the back of his neck, his elbow propped on his bent knee. "She recovered, as was promised. And that's when she told me she was in love with someone else. Had been since before we were married. They'd planned to run off together before she fell ill."

I waited for him to rail against the unfairness he'd been dealt, rage against the betrayal, but he spoke as though it were simple fact. Like it had happened to someone else.

Maybe it was so long ago, it seemed like it had.

"You didn't have any idea?"

"None. I was in love with her. So deeply I obviously missed how alone I was in my feelings. Anyway, they left, I got sick— and no one was there to barter for me."

Pain hugged my insides. I found myself wanting to go to him, but his closed posture kept me where I was.

Finally, his gaze returned to mine. "I ran from the world, Katerina, and I stayed hidden for five hundred years. You—" He stopped and cleared his throat. "You will find your way through this. With time. With some new purpose. It will get better."

My vision blurred again, and my throat ached with the effort of holding back my tears, but I wouldn't let them fall. He was right. I was torturing myself by day even as my dreams tormented me by night, and none of it helped to put what had happened behind me.

Perhaps looking to the future was the only way forward, as terrifying a thought as it was.

Questions bubbled on my tongue, wanting to know more about his life before, the terms of his deal, his wishes and regrets—but the same respect for his privacy kept me quiet. He'd trusted me with this much. We had an eternity for him to decide to tell me more.

"Come." He pushed himself to his feet. "We'll find a place to have a real meal tonight. Get dressed and we'll go."

He stepped through the mist, leaving me alone to dry myself and put on the clean clothes he'd brought me, and reappeared shortly after to lead me away from the sea and towards our next destination.

7

Katerina

France - June 1207

WHEN WE'D CROSSED the channel into Calais so many years ago, I'd felt like a weight had been lifted off my shoulders. The language was different, the scenery was different, and with the changes, I'd stopped looking up every time I heard a voice that sounded like my husband's or my father's. I'd stopped hoping to catch the faintest hint of a northern accent that would bring my thoughts to home.

That relief only grew the farther south we went, though as the years passed, Emrick seemed to grow more tense.

"What is it?" I asked one night after we'd stopped to rest at yet another alehouse, this one so like the many others we'd stayed at I forgot where we were.

"Don't you feel it?" He stood at the barn door, his narrowed eyes watching, one hand resting over his other glove. His thumb ran under the hem as though he were braced to tear the glove off and send someone to an early grave. "The farther south we go, the heavier the air becomes. Like there's a storm brewing."

I didn't notice, but after the many centuries he'd been around, his senses were better attuned to such changes. It made sense, as those changes often meant death.

For nine years we wandered France, always heading south, staying a few months here, a few months there, with no clear destination in mind, but now, at least, a goal of learning and absorbing the shifts in culture as we travelled.

Rumours followed us of trouble stirring in the Languedoc region of southern France, lands that claimed a certain amount of independence from the north. There were religious and political grumblings. Stories of rising crime as mercenaries swept through the area, uncontrolled by the divided lords.

Emrick suggested we detour west, but I insisted we continue south. Languedoc had become widely recognized as a place of tolerance, allowing people with new ideas and faiths to live comfortably beside one another.

What better place for a sorceress without home or family and only a servant of Death for companionship?

When we reached the busy port town of Montpellier,

however, Emrick stayed close by my side, his mercurial eyes growing darker, his shoulders higher, his posture stiffer whenever anyone eyed me a moment too long.

I did my best to pay attention and try to figure out for myself what had him on edge, but aside from the preachers loudly proclaiming against the so-called Good Christians, the heretics that had become a blight on the country, I didn't notice anything.

"What rot," Emrick said as he turned his back on another priest raving to a group gathered outside the church.

"What is it?" I looked over my shoulder to make out what the man was saying as Emrick hooked his hand under my elbow to lead me away.

"Zealous men being zealots," he said. "Always working to stir up conflict between people while claiming to want to bring them together. It seems they've found a new target."

"Oh?"

"It doesn't matter. Just more reason to keep moving before trouble comes so we don't wind up getting involved."

That was something I'd come to expect from Emrick—his detachment. Even as he encouraged me to return to the world, he increased his distance from it. I often envied his ability to step into the afterlife and leave everything behind him whenever he chose.

It was to be expected, I supposed, from someone who no

longer stood with both feet in the mortal world.

Sort of like me now.

Yet I couldn't walk away the way he did. During all my years in Palonia, I'd never believed I would get a chance to see the world for myself. Now that I was here, I found myself devouring knowledge. I soaked up the language, remembering the lessons Shep had taught me when he returned from his travels, late nights lying in bed, limbs entwined, as he tried to teach me the fundamentals of languages from around the world. The way he used to laugh at my accent.

I wondered if he'd be proud to know I now spoke French fluently enough to be considered one of them as I made my way through this pocket of the continent.

The thought was bittersweet, and I hugged my cloak tighter around myself as Emrick led us into an inn in the centre of town.

The moment we passed through the door, he stopped and stiffened. Then he turned on his heel and led us back out, down the road, and into the empty stretch of forest that wrapped around the city.

"We'll spend the night here, but tomorrow we should leave," he said as I lit a fire.

"Why? You've been speaking of this place for weeks as somewhere we might stay for a while."

Although the idea of staying in one spot long enough for

people to ask me questions about myself had terrified me the first time we'd done it, I'd begun to look forward to it. To set down roots, if only for a few months or years before our lack of aging made it necessary for us to move on.

"The vibration in the air bothers me. Some kind of magic, like a scent of rot. Pervasive and foul, but impossible to root out the source."

My interest perked up. "Magic? What sort of magic?"

So far on our travels, we hadn't encountered much outside the mundane. Emrick had done his best to keep me away from it. On my own, with so little ability to defend myself, I would be easy pickings for most magicals looking to fight.

As for the sorcerers, staying away from them had been my decision. I still didn't have the stomach to explain to my own kind what had happened to Palonia. Not only for fear of being an object of pity, but also for the chance they'd reject me for my unintentional immortality.

"I can't place it," he said. "But it's dark. Tainted." His eyes narrowed. "It reminds me of the way Palonia felt that night."

A shudder ran through me, and I wrapped my arms around my middle. I wished I could feel it for myself, but the only sensations I experienced when I closed my eyes were the soft breeze brushing against my skin and the scratch of grass beneath my legs.

If I'd been travelling with my family—and properly

trained—our first priority would have been routing this dark magic out and destroying it. That had been our purpose, our way of keeping our region and our people safe.

On my own, however, I had nothing to offer except wishing things were different.

"Is there no way to help?" I asked.

His moonlight gaze ran over me. "You know I can't."

I sighed. "I know. You can't interfere with the lives of mortals."

"However much I wish I could," he said. "There are consequences for disrupting the natural balance."

I supposed I understood, but it didn't seem fair that two people with a certain amount of power could do nothing to stand in the way of those wishing to cause harm.

What was the point of living forever if a person couldn't invest herself in the world? Was this what I had to look forward to? Noticing problems and leaving them to be someone else's responsibility?

Covering my heart in frost like I had my body, protecting myself while everyone else suffered?

For sixty years, that had been enough for me, but, for reasons I couldn't explain, that stopped tonight. Emrick was limited by the terms of his deal with Death, but I wasn't. This was still my world, and I had an opportunity to do what I'd failed to do in Palonia: help.

My pulse leapt at the idea of standing on my own against whatever threat Emrick sensed. Staring into the unknown, aware of the danger, wanting to run but unwilling to do it.

Swallowing my fear, I drew my shoulders back. "I'm going to stay."

Emrick stiffened. "You're what?"

I nodded, steeling my resolve. "I'm going to stay. If something is happening here, I want to know what it is. Help where I can, even if it's only in small ways." My shoulders slumped. "I'm tired, Emrick. Not of the wandering, but of having no purpose. I don't want to spend eternity feeling like a speck of dust drifting in the air. I want to put down new roots."

"Katerina…" The sympathy in his eyes turned my stomach. "Unless you find a place filled with immortals, you'll always be uprooted, and every time you are, your heart will break. Is that really what you want?"

I appreciated where he was coming from, but his argument fell flat on my ears. "I've already lost the one person in the universe I should have given my life to save. After that pain, I think I can tolerate a few goodbyes."

He jerked his chin in acknowledgement, but his gaze never left mine. "You know I can't stay with you."

My heart squeezed, but I breathed through the moment of panic. He'd left me alone often enough when we stopped somewhere for a few months. His inability to involve himself meant it was easiest for him to be away. I understood that and what it meant for me. But I could be strong enough to exist without him. I had never been the sort to depend wholly on anyone else, and I'd come to rely far too heavily on Emrick's company.

This would be a positive change.

"I'd come see you," he added. "If you wanted me to."

The panic softened under a blanket of relief, although it didn't abate altogether. "I'd like that. Thank you."

He looked around, his gaze falling onto the flames as they licked the night air. "I suppose there's no reason for me to stay any longer." He returned his attention to me. "Unless you want me to? For the night, I mean. So you can sleep."

I stared back at him, my heart racing at the thought of him walking away. I struggled to picture making decisions without his input, making my way forward without his guidance.

He would be back eventually, but until then I had no way to contact him, and even if I did, what could he do to help me if I got in over my head with this dark magic?

The urge to accept his offer was strong. His presence had become as important to me as my family's had ever been.

But if he stayed tonight, he would still be here tomorrow, and if he offered to stay tomorrow, I doubted I would have the courage to send him away then, and if I didn't find my courage, I might as well march right out of Languedoc and keep walking.

If I wanted to make a difference, I had to let go.

"No," I made myself say. "I'll be all right."

I couldn't tell if he was disappointed. Sixty years together, and I still felt as though I barely knew him. He pushed himself to his feet and summoned the mists that would take him away from me. "Very well. I'll check in on you when I can. Be safe, Katerina. History has a way of sneaking up on you before you realize it's happening."

Before I could change my mind and beg him to stay, he stepped backwards into the afterlife and was gone.

8

Katerina

Montpellier, France - November 1208

EVEN WITHOUT EMRICK'S ability to sense the dark magic on the air, I understood all was not well in this region of France.

Mercenaries, the primary force of law, prowled the streets with no one to stand against them. I avoided them well enough, but it was more of a challenge to ignore the spiritual tension lingering in the air.

The lord of the region had stepped back, allowing the Good Christians and the priests to tend to their own, and the result was a battle of wills that ran along the earth, trembling the soles of my boots.

The heretical sect had been a growing threat to the Catholic Church for decades. I'd heard about them with increasing frequency the farther south we'd travelled, and in this self-contained part of the world, they'd been left to carry out their lives without anyone hindering their beliefs or practices.

Not that the indifference of the people stopped many a priest from spouting their fear-mongering sermons from the pulpit, accusing the Good Christians of blaspheming God.

Appeals to the Pope had been made to step in and banish this heresy from the region, and I'd been around long enough to know that rarely ended well. The effects of the earlier Crusades were long-lasting and widespread, and I feared what might come if the matter wasn't settled quickly.

I remained in Montpellier for over a year, playing the role of a widow who had lost her husband to war. Being a woman alone came with no small amount of judgement, but I tried to keep to myself and put my faith in the innkeeper's need for coin to help me fend off unwanted attention.

At the same time, I searched for the source of the magic Emrick had sensed, wandering the city and the woods beyond it or following the priests filled with their twisted words, all to no avail. Every once in a while, when the voices of the priests and their followers grew louder against the heretics, I thought I sensed the darkness Emrick had described, but it faded too quickly for me to track it.

I wished Emrick could have stayed with me. Although I was surrounded by people, and the energy of the bustling town was soothing to my lonely soul, I found myself feeling more isolated and alone among the crowds than I had by myself in the woods. I missed the spirit-herder's quiet presence. The way he tried, ever so subtly, to make me smile. The softness of his gaze on me when he thought I didn't notice.

His absence left a gnawing hole in my soul, as though he'd taken a piece of me with him. Which I supposed was true given the bond that tied us together.

Part of me was surprised he'd stayed away for a whole year, but the other part of me accepted it as confirmation of the suspicions I'd long held—that he'd been waiting for an excuse to return to his life and leave me behind.

The thought shouldn't have hurt, and I did my best to ignore the pinch of regret, knowing I'd made the best decision for me, but as autumn came and slowly made its way to winter, I found myself unable to stay where I was. Not only did staying here reinforce my constant hope for Emrick's return, but it was a daily remainder of my failure to uproot the evil that had snared the region.

So, finally, I left, once more setting out without any destination in mind.

Doubt assailed me as I followed the road. Perhaps Emrick had the right of it in staying detached from this world. With my magic at my fingertips and the ability to heal from any serious injury, I wasn't concerned about my physical wellbeing, but there was still so much I didn't know, and although I couldn't die, that didn't mean I couldn't suffer. Or that the coin Emrick and I had gathered and saved couldn't be lost, leaving me without food, clothing, or a roof over my head. New places would mean new stories about why I travelled alone, always gaining attention, always raising suspicion.

Which made me all the more frustrated that Emrick had refused to help me develop my magic and all the more determined to teach myself. The foundational knowledge had been drilled into me since I was a child, and with every opportunity, I put it to work. So far, I'd noticed no progress, and with every new failure, I became more certain of my brokenness, but I didn't intend to let that stop me.

On my second day of travels, my thoughts were interrupted by the heavy hoofbeats of a runaway beast being chased by a young man in a monk's robes.

"Stop that horse!" he shouted, his hand raised in the air, his face red and sweaty.

I leapt to grab the rope attached to the creature's harness as it flew past me, grateful to be wearing my leather gloves as the rough fibres tore across my palms.

The nag protested the sharp stop, but she bent her nose into my outstretched hand as I shared a bite of apple I'd been saving for dinner.

The monk reached my side and bent at the waist, his hands on his knees, his breath coming in heavy gasps. Slowly, he straightened, and I handed him the rope.

"I appreciate your assistance," he said, still a bit wheezy. "I would have hated to lose the precious cargo she carries."

"Treasure?" I teased.

"To me, yes. In the form of books."

I looked him over. He was about thirty years old, average-looking, with thinning dark hair, squinty brown eyes, and the sort of pale skin that suggested he didn't often see much sunlight. He might have been tall, but his shoulders were too stooped to get a clear idea. A scribe, I guessed.

"You're a scholar, then?"

"I am. Brother Godfrey, madame. I study religious texts and make copies for the Church. Anything to preserve the word of our Lord and help us spread His message."

I pressed my lips together and offered a polite bow. "Then I'm glad I caught her. I wish you a good day."

I prepared to continue my walk down the road, but to my dismay, the man kept pace with me. The last thing I wanted on my travels was to be stuck with a priest who spewed the same rantings and ravings as those I'd left behind, but I had no excuse to send him on his way.

"You're heading to Béziers?" he asked, squinting at me. I

wasn't sure if it was out of judgement or simply to see me better.

"I am." I hadn't been, but if he knew of a place down this road where I could eat and sleep on a halfway decent bed, all the better.

"Then I wonder if you'd give me permission to walk with you. This region is not safe for a young woman to go alone. There are mercenaries everywhere. Even me, a man of God, has had trouble with them."

He scowled and adjusted his homespun robes.

"My husband was a soldier. He was lost to the Crusades, but not before he taught me how to defend myself."

"A questionable skill for a young woman to have, but I suppose, under the circumstances, a wise one. Power is slipping in all corners of Languedoc, and I fear what will become of my home."

"I've heard much talk of the heretics causing distress to the Church. They're the reason for the increase in mercenaries, are they not?"

His expression grew dark, and I braced myself for a lecture on the evils of the rising sect. "The heretics are a symptom of something much worse than earthly power."

Despite myself, my interest piqued. That was far from the answer I'd expected. "How so?"

"They are evidence of a demonic presence oozing through

our world, stirring up trouble where none existed before."

I didn't know whether to laugh or pay attention. "You believe the Good Christians are driven by demons?"

His eyebrows climbed halfway up his forehead. "No, madame, I believe the heretics are driven by ignorance, as are all who follow the path away from the true Church. I speak of the growing fear *against* the heretics."

I drew to a stop and turned to face him. "What do you mean?"

"Whispers in the ears of my fellow brothers and the priests who lead the faithful, warning them of the dangers these heretics bring, how they'll strip the power of the Church if left unchecked. Lies, of course. The Church is too strong a force to be brought down by some murmurings of equality. The only explanation for how quickly these heated feelings and words have spread against these people is that some evil force lurks behind them."

"Forgive me, Brother Godfrey, but doesn't the Church claim its role is to weed out heresy and protect the souls of the faithful?"

He dropped his chin in a solemn nod. "It is, and sometimes our leaders must be forceful, but this"—he waved his hand at the world—"this encouragement to terrorize one's brothers and sisters, of advocating widespread violence among our neighbours—it seems to me to go against the basic tenets of our beliefs. If there's no one behind the trouble created by the Church, then the trouble comes from within the Church itself, which I refuse to believe. But for a Papal Bull to be signed? For soldiers to be ordered against our own people? It goes too far."

I bit my tongue to hold back my opinions of his Church and asked, "Do your fellow brothers agree with you?"

He snorted. "Of course not. They accuse me of walking too closely to the heretical line myself by speaking against His Holiness's orders. It's why they encouraged me to take this journey to deliver these books and assist the priests of Béziers in protecting our Catholic brethren." He looked over his shoulder as though to confirm we were alone and, in a lower voice, said, "But I have seen them."

I dropped my volume to match his. "The demons?"

"No, the people who summoned them. Nobles from the north. People angry at the power shift the Good Christians bring with them. With some of my fellow priests spurring them on."

It sounded like nonsense, and I was tempted to disregard his ravings as those of a secluded man more focused on inks and vellum than the world, but Emrick's warning echoed in my ears. His sense of something dark and tainted crossing the country. Would demons explain it?

I made a note to ask him when—if—he came back, but for now allowed Godfrey to continue his tale, describing the hooded figures creeping through the woods, standing around a fire, whispering to each other over old texts that reeked of demonic energies. His details grew increasingly vague, and I suspected much of what he said was the result of too much time with his imagination. Even so, I stored the knowledge, wanting to be sure I had it available to call back whenever Emrick returned. If he did.

Or—and despite my purpose for the last year, this thought terrified me—if I encountered this demon for myself.

9

Katerina

WE ARRIVED IN Béziers late the next day.

Despite the hour, the streets were full of people coming and going, hailing their neighbours as they returned home or carousing down the street as they made their way from one alehouse to the next.

It was a city that radiated the energy of its people, and I was immediately drawn to it.

As a port town, Montpellier had welcomed folk from all places and backgrounds, but Béziers was a community. I saw proof of it in the groups that passed me with laughter and smiles and in the crowds gathered at the market stalls sharing gossip.

Despite the good cheer, however, tension had followed us into the city. I caught more than one person eying me warily, taking in my clean, simple dress, my worn shoes, my single sack of belongings. I was an unknown in a town where everyone knew each other, at a time when the Church was commanding people to be watchful of their neighbours.

The place smelled of fear hidden behind bright smiles, and I didn't know if they were afraid *of* me or *for* me.

Was it possible the dark magic Emrick had sensed had already made its way here, burrowing into the hearts of these people, spreading like an unseen sickness until it reached a breaking point?

I worried I'd made a mistake following Godfrey. Or perhaps the mistake had been leaving Montpellier. Or letting Emrick walk away. I had no idea how to navigate this potential conflict.

My doubts increased as a group of large men in tattered leathers armed to the teeth closed in around Godfrey and me. The other people on the street flowed around us as though they didn't see what was happening, and I wished their voluntary blindness would extend to me using my magic.

Unfortunately, the odds were slim that no one would notice four men spontaneously catching fire, and I didn't want Godfrey suspecting the demon he feared might in fact be me.

"What you got in those bags?" one of the men asked,

leering at Godfrey as he pawed at the satchel hooked over the nag's back.

"Or we could take the horse," said another.

"I'd rather have some time with this bit right here." The third man stepped closer to me and hooked his fingers beneath the belt at my waist to keep me from running.

Rage that I was stuck in this position with no way to defend myself thrashed within me. Emrick's knife sat at my hip, but there was no way one blade would help me against four men, and I doubted Godfrey was in any position to fight them off.

The mercenary closed his fist around my belt and pushed me backwards into a reeking alley. My boot stuck in a muddy puddle, and cold water leaked through my worn sole to soak my stocking.

Once I was out of view of the street, the thug shoved me hard, sending me flying onto my back. My shoulder blades crunched against stone, and I swallowed a scream, refusing to give him the satisfaction. Instinctively, my hands warmed as magic raced through my blood, swelling in my palms, and I willed it back before anyone noticed.

Godfrey protested as another man put his thick arm around his chest to hold him off. The nag ran, taking the monk's books with him, and I suspected the brother's pain over his loss was greater than his concern for my safety.

"You want to die today, priest?" one of the men asked.

"N-no, of course not."

"Then shut your mouth and give us your purse."

Godfrey did as he demanded, and the man shoved him away. "Get ye gone. If you run fast enough, maybe you'll catch up with that near-dead horse of yours."

The monk spared me a look, and I silently bade him run. He would be safer for leaving, and I would be free to unleash my fire. The mercenaries might have thought they were being smart by getting me out of view, but they had no way of knowing they'd sealed their fates.

Godfrey hesitated, and in the space of a second, the thug on top of me slammed my head against the ground. Stars flashed in my vision, and I cursed the monk's reticence to leave me.

When two of the men crowded him again, however, he turned and fled, leaving me alone with them. The man on top of me shifted his weight, his meaty fingers clawing at my skirts, and I bared my teeth and summoned my fire to the surface.

Before I had a chance to unleash it, a booming voice filled the alley.

"You lot! Clear off!"

As one, the four men turned to stare at the even larger man standing behind them. He held a raised stick in his hand and didn't hesitate to brandish it, hitting first one man, then another. In the distraction, I pulled the dagger from the sheath at my hip and jammed it into the shoulder of the mercenary on top of me. He cried out and backhanded me across the cheek but didn't have time to strike me again before that stick came down on his head.

A rough hand reached out for me, and I grabbed it, using the stranger's strength to pull myself up.

"Hurry, madame," he said. "Come with me."

I didn't think twice about following him, not knowing where else to go and confident that, stick aside, I could take him if he decided to pick up where the mercenaries had left off. With my grip tight around the hilt of Emrick's knife, I stepped lightly around the groaning men at my feet.

We hurriedly left the alley, and he led me along the side streets into a quiet row of cramped houses where he finally slowed.

"My apologies, Madame…"

I took in his appearance, the greying stubble along his jaw, the kind brown eyes lined with deep wrinkles in the corners, his shaved head showing sprouts of grey amongst the brown. He couldn't have been more than forty-five, roughened by labour but hanging on to a youthfulness that belied the wear and tear of life.

"Palon," I said. "Katerina Palon."

"Madame Palon. I would have stepped in sooner, but I had to find a suitable weapon."

He chucked the stick into the front garden of one of the houses and turned to me with a wide smile.

"I'm grateful you stepped in when you did, monsieur. I doubt I could have gotten them to stop on my own."

Not with witnesses, anyway.

"Jean Artois, at your service," he said with a slight bow. "Brewer of Béziers, owner of the finest alehouse this side of Lyon. If you'll permit me to escort you home, I'll have Edith— my lovely wife—see to your wounds before you continue on your way."

I blinked at the rapid transition from introduction to invitation and looked over my shoulder to see how far we'd come from where I'd left Godfrey. "I don't suppose you saw what happened to the monk I travelled with?"

"He must have already left. I can have my son inquire at the Cathedral for him to ensure he arrived safely if you wish."

"That's very kind, thank you."

The man offered me his arm, and, having no reason not to go with him, I accepted it. My only other option was to seek refuge in the church hostel, which had never been my preferred accommodation.

"These *routiers* have gotten out of control," Jean grumbled as we walked. "But with all eyes turned to the soldiers marching in our direction, no one is willing to step in to stop them."

"Soldiers?"

"Oui, madame. It seems our Cathari neighbours have riled the wrong feathers, and those up north are determined to root them out. Unfortunate for them they'll find no welcome in Béziers."

"Oh?"

"Here, we protect our own."

He winked at me and steered me towards the alehouse that stood a little apart from its crowded neighbours up ahead. A barn stood next to the house, three horses poking their noses out, suggesting business tonight was good, and raucous noise came from within.

The shift from cool evening to crowded interior hit me with heat from the blaze in the hearth and the smell of sweat and horse and cooked stew. The tables were filled, and more than one man lay on the floor, but the atmosphere was relaxed and homey.

"Jean, is that you?" a woman called as she came out from the back room. At least half her husband's age, her eyes were as bright as her smile, her voice warm. She wore her hair pulled back under a kerchief to keep it out of her face, though a few blonde strands flew free. Her hands and apron were covered in flour, and sweat glistened on her brow. "There you are. You're so late, I was worried."

He put his arm around his wife's shoulders and angled her towards me. "Edith, this is Madame Katerina Palon. I saved her from some mercenaries looking to mar the friendly reputation of our town."

Edith snorted. "Reputation is all it is these days." She turned her sympathetic eyes on me. "I trust you're unhurt?"

"Thanks to your husband, yes."

Jean glanced at my forehead and his brow furrowed in confusion. "I could have sworn—"

I brushed my hair over where the wound had been. "It was just a scrape, I think. Looked worse than it was."

Jean's expression cleared as though my explanation was enough to return the world to its rightful place, as most mundanes did when faced with mysteries they couldn't explain. "I brought her here so she can wash away the effects of the attack. I trust you won't mind helping her?"

Without balking at any extra work or inconvenience, Edith smiled and hooked her arm under mine. "Of course. Come with me away from the rabble out here." She projected her voice so the rabble in question would hear her, and they waved her away with laughs as she led me through the door into the back room.

Here it was quieter if more stifling for the lack of open doors. The woodstove sent heavy smoke billowing outwards, warming the room against the cooler night air.

"The children are asleep," Edith said, dropping her voice, "but we have space enough for you to wash." She cast me a sidelong glance from under her long lashes. "You travel alone?"

"My husband died in the Crusades not long ago. I only just arrived in Béziers."

"With no place to stay?"

When I shook my head, she straightened and took both my hands in her calloused ones. "Then you'll stay here as long as you need. We'll find room for you."

Warmth spread through my chest, and I swallowed the lump that formed in my throat.

This gentle contact from a stranger and her soft, generous words brought me closer to home than anything else had in sixty years.

And if my suspicions were correct, everything about this place was at risk thanks to a growing malignant force that threatened to suck the kindness out of these people.

So far, Béziers hadn't shown me much worth saving, but for the two people in this house, my resolve hardened to investigate Godfrey's suspicions and Emrick's worries. My skills weren't strong, but my drive was, and I prayed to the gods it would be enough to keep these people safe and help me take a step towards redemption.

10

Emrick

Béziers, France - July 1209

I STEPPED OUT of the afterlife to find Katerina standing beside the river along the shore opposite town, trying hard to throw a lick of flame from her palm into the murky water below. Every time she released the fire, it sputtered into nothing, and after the fifth attempt, she stomped her foot in frustration.

By the red tint on the back of her neck and the flush of her cheeks, I suspected she'd been out here for hours, and by her expression, I guessed those hours had been to no benefit.

As I watched her try again and again, memories swept over me of my own practice over five centuries ago in a village even smaller than Palonia had been. I remembered the power that had surged through my veins and strengthened my muscles. The confidence that came with the ability to bend the air to my will and create ripples across the lake.

Seeing her try and fail, I immediately saw where her trouble lay. Her magic was strong, her form perfect—it was the mental blocks that prevented her from projecting her power and becoming the full sorceress she was born to be. She didn't believe she was capable of harbouring such power in her small body. Or perhaps it was the heaviness of expectation she'd absorbed as a child, making her feel she'd never achieve the level of perfection her parents and teachers wanted. It was clear enough how terrified she was of failure.

I found myself overwhelmed by the desire to make her see her own potential.

But I also knew what helping her would mean. It would risk another piece of my soul if Death perceived my assistance as meddlesome. I'd already given up a few for the sake of this woman. At the rate I was going, I would lose everything that remained of me and become nothing more than a mindless wraith before the end of the century.

Almost more frightening was the idea of spending time with her in close proximity, getting to know her as more than just the tormented woman I'd guided away from her night-mares.

It would risk the walls I'd built around my heart, walls I

would not tear down simply because this lost soul had been bound to me against her will.

Even if she was the most beautiful, stubborn, and alluring creature I'd encountered in centuries.

Especially because she was.

I'd spent my two years away from her hoping to break this hold she had over me, but all I'd done was think of her. More than once, I'd skirted the mists, watching her from the afterlife to ensure she was safe. More than once, I'd had to hold myself back from reaching out to her, wanting to ease her nightmares or clear the furrow from her brow.

I'd done my best, and although I wasn't yet ready to give up, I couldn't bring myself to stay away after what I'd learned of the danger creeping towards Béziers. Katerina sat directly in the path of a brewing war and had no idea it was coming.

That was the only reason I was here. To warn her. I swore it to myself.

Resolve renewed, I stepped into the world. Her eyes widened on seeing me, and although she immediately returned her attention to her practice, her cheekbones flushed pink.

"I thought you'd forgotten about me," she said. Her tone was indifferent, but I sensed the weight of her words.

I couldn't tamp down the smile that wrestled on my lips. "It's only been two years."

"Two years is a decent span when you're stuck walking the

earth."

"Give it time and you'll lose track as often as I do. Every day feels like an eternity, while a century might pass in an hour."

"How confusing. No wonder you're always so grim."

I crossed my arms and watched as she summoned another flame into her palm. This one she managed to grow into a decent sized fireball, but again when she released it, it fizzled into nothing.

"Curse the spirits," she hissed, and drew more fire between her fingers.

I found myself captivated by the adorable crease between her brows and the faint pout of her lips as discouragement overcame her, and despite all my arguments to stay out of it, I closed the distance between us.

One small piece of advice wouldn't lead to my destruction.

"You're dropping your magic too soon. Wait until you lose contact with the flame before you null the power."

She shot me a side-eyed glance and did as I suggested, drawing fire into her palm and holding it there for a moment before slowly pulling her hand back and miming her throw. The flame bounced like a rubber ball into the river. Her blue eyes sparkled with pride and glee, an expression I'd never seen before, and immediately I ached to see it more often.

Too soon, her joy vanished under a pinch of grief, and she raised her gaze to mine. "Thank you."

I swallowed to remind my tongue how to function. "You're welcome."

My heart pounded steadily and loudly in my ears for a few extra beats before she finally looked away and cleared her throat.

"Is this the reason you came back?" She hurled another fireball into the water, this time with much more heft behind her throw as she found confidence in her magic. "Did you change your mind about teaching me?"

I wished that was why I'd come back. Life would be easier and my worries would be less if all I had to contend with was her lacklustre power.

"I came to suggest you leave this place. France in general, but Languedoc specifically."

Another fireball landed in the water and vanished in smoke. "Oh? Why is that?"

"That magic I warned you about—it's spreading. My duties have kept me crossing from border to border, and the reek of evil is overwhelming. Whatever is causing the fear to grow against this religious group, it's becoming more potent, choking reason, compassion—sanity, even."

She snuck me a look from behind her long black hair before another fireball formed in her palm. This one she held on to, spinning it in tight circles until the orange-red ball turned white-hot before she released it. I was impressed when it didn't fly from her hand right away but hovered an inch above her palm. A convenient trick, that, if you were stuck in a dark place. When her control slipped and the ball nearly unravelled, she threw it in the river and watched it sizzle into nothing.

"I've done a fair bit of searching on my own, but the source of this magic eludes me," she said. "What have you heard?"

I crossed my arms and leaned against the shaded tree beside me. I hated that she was still poking around in the matter. I'd hoped that after so long without success, she would have given up. With luck, the news I brought would make her realize the danger she was in. "The soldiers are marching, Kat. The Pope has sanctioned his knights to hunt down and slaughter any heretic or sympathizer. In another few weeks, it won't be safe for you here."

"It's Kate," she corrected. "And I know. I've been here for eight months, and the tensions have risen beyond the point of comfort. But I'm not leaving."

I clenched my teeth and squeezed my hands into fists, hidden beneath my crossed arms. "What do you mean you're not leaving? If you know—"

"These people need help, Emrick. Why do you think I'm here trying to figure out how to do more than make my fingers glow? I'd be a lot farther along if you'd given me that tip two years ago."

"You think you can staunch the tide of an entire Crusade?"

The look she shot me over her shoulder might have quelled a less desperate man. "Are you saying I can't?"

"The soldiers are torturing people. Slaughtering them in horrible, excruciating ways with the claim of purifying their souls. They won't turn around and leave because a single woman stands in their way and tells them they're not wanted."

She didn't need to know the carnage and cruelty I'd witnessed over the past few years. Nothing I hadn't seen before over the course of my tenure as spiritual escort, but more personal this time due to the involvement of this woman.

Whether I wished I could swear off her company or not, I couldn't bear the thought of any harm coming to her. If I thought it would help, I would whisk her to safety, but somehow I suspected she would fight her way back.

Instead of arguing with me, she let her last fireball wither on her palm, wiped her hands on her apron, and stepped towards me. With a quick look over her shoulder and in a voice so low I had to bow my head to hear her, she asked, "What do you know of demons?"

I started, that being the last question I'd expected. "Why?"

She shrugged and played with a loose thread on her belt. "I met this monk on my way here, and he suspected demonic influence behind the Church's response to these Good Christians. I haven't been able to learn anything else, but does that fit with what you sense?"

The acid in my stomach bubbled and churned, rising to burn the back of my throat. "It does. It would explain quite a bit, actually, and it's all the more reason for you to say goodbye to these people while you can. The soldiers are closing in, the fear coming with them like a noxious cloud, and if you get caught in it—"

She looked up at me sharply. "What can they do to me, Emrick? Kill me? Perhaps I should let them try and see how they get on."

"We don't know how far your immortality extends. It's possible they could succeed, but their success would be neither quick nor merciful. You would suffer more than you can possibly imagine."

"Then perhaps my debt might finally be paid."

She spat the words out as a quick retort, but the speed with which she turned her back on me made me think she hadn't intended to say them aloud. I inched closer to her, inhaled her scent of pine and sun. "You owe nothing, Katerina. Not to the world, and not to those you've lost. Is sixty years not enough to make you see how innocent you are in what happened?"

"A thousand years wouldn't be enough." Her voice was rough as she bowed her head. "I stood by while Alodie, Mae, and Blythe tore my family from me. I saved myself while everyone I loved suffered. No amount of time can make up for my failure to act." Her back stiffened, and she raised her head, staring out across the river to the city filled with people who had no idea of the danger hanging over their heads. "In the months I've been here, I've seen how these people care for each other. They understand family and community. More than anywhere else I've been since—" Her voice caught, and she tightened her fists to summon her strength. "They won't turn on each other no matter what the Pope orders them to do, and if I can stand between the demon and them, I will."

"You'll fail."

She turned to face me, and if she was startled by my closeness, she didn't show it. "Then I fail. But at least I'll have tried."

Her chin rose in determination, her ocean eyes raging, threatening to pull me into the current, leaving me breathless. I stared down at her, overcome by the urge—the *need*—to run my fingers along her cheek. To capture her chin between my fingers, lean down, and—

I stopped myself before I imagined claiming her lips with mine. That was too far. Too much.

Instead, I stepped away, my chest filled with frustration and not a little sorrow. "You know I can't involve myself in the fates of mortals, Kate. The demon might have stepped from the infernal realms, but a mortal summoned it. I can't help you."

She squeezed her hands at her sides, no less defiant than she'd been a moment ago. A queen. A goddess. Even if she was terrified. "I'm not asking for your help. I may be bound to you,

Emrick, but I'm not dependent on you. I'm more than willing to fight this battle myself."

Fear for her caught in my throat, and I dropped my head in a nod. "Can I say nothing to stop you?"

Her lips wobbled, but she shook her head. "Nothing."

Buried under the weight of resignation, I sighed and my shoulders slumped. "Some advice, then. The demon has likely taken a host, a human body to hide its true face. Unfortunately for them, mortal bodies can't contain that much power, so they rot quickly. To kill the demon, you'll need its blood. The easiest way is to kill the host, which can't be saved anyway, and as soon as the demon leaves, you strike. With its blood, all you need to do is see him and speak the words to send it back to the infernal realms."

I gave her the words and made her repeat them back to me until they rolled strong and clear from her perfect mouth.

"He might also try to take over your body," I warned. "You're a powerful magic user, and more than that, you're immortal. As his host, you would be able to carry him indef- initely—a rare enough phenomenon that he won't pass up the opportunity to claim you. Stay aware and keep your mind closed. He cannot take what is not given, so imagine your mind as a trap that cannot be opened no matter how hard he works to find his way in."

Fear drifted across her eyes, but she nodded her understanding without putting her worries into words.

It was all I could do, no matter how badly I wanted to offer more.

My heart ached. Arguments pooled on my lips to try to convince her to swear off this task she'd assigned herself, but I swallowed them as a waste of breath. I had no claim on her or her decisions. Whatever she chose, she would have to accept the consequences.

"I wish you luck," I said. "I hope to see you again once this is over."

But there was no guarantee. Not against a demon.

In so many ways, my life would be easier if she failed. Once again, I would have no ties to this world. I could return to being alone in the universe with only my debt to carry until it was finally paid.

Her eyes followed me as I stepped through the mist, and I wondered if I would ever see that blaze of sapphire again.

11

Katerina

IF EMRICK THOUGHT to scare me away from Béziers with his warning, he failed.

Even so, I wished he could have stayed with me. I hadn't been able to shake the way he'd stared at me as we stood alone beside the river, so close together. The intensity—the depth of his moonlight eyes. My flesh had ached to close the gap between us, as though the magic that bound us called for me to lose myself in his company.

But I wasn't ready to lose myself. Not until I'd made an attempt to remove the threat to the Artois family and everyone else in this city that in so many ways reminded me of home.

"All is well, Katerina?" Edith asked when I returned to the house. "Your face is red."

I pressed my hands to my cheeks, their warmth soaking into my fingers. "Too much sun. I'll be all right in a moment."

"Let me fetch you some wine." She started to rise from where she peeled potatoes at the table, her swollen stomach giving away the progress of the latest addition to the family, and I waved her back down.

"I can fetch my own, though I might go back out and take a walk. It's such a beautiful day that it would be a shame to waste it inside. Can I fetch you anything from the market?"

Edith's kind face twisted with concern. "Are you sure it's wise for you to spend so much time on your own? You know these streets are less safe now than when you arrived."

It was true the mercenary bands had become more brutal with every passing month, spurred on by the distraction of their lords as soldiers, mercenaries, and followers of the faith marched south. I didn't fear them, however. Emrick's lesson by the river had raised my confidence in my magic, and I was certain I could fend them off.

"I won't be long. I'll see if there's any fresh cabbage to be had."

"Won't you at least wait for Jean to return?"

I rested my hand over hers. "Don't fret, Edith. I'm not going far."

I grabbed my hat from beside my cot and headed out again, this time striking for l'Eglise de la Madeleine, the beautiful cathedral that dominated Béziers. With Emrick's confirmation that we were likely looking at a demon, the news of the approaching soldiers, and my newfound skill with my magic, I was finally ready to begin an active search for the evil stalking the streets, and the only person who might help me lived within these thick stone walls.

In all my time here, I hadn't sought out Brother Godfrey. Any frustration I'd felt towards him for not running away faster had subsided, but until I was prepared to face this demon, there hadn't been much point in taking him away from his studies. Not when asking him to elaborate on his suspicions might direct some of them my way.

After all, who was I but a slight young woman making her way in a man's world? But I hoped his desire to share his beliefs would override any concern he had over the inappropriateness of my interest.

When I stepped into the cathedral, the sudden removal of the bright afternoon sun sent a chill skittering down my back. The thin soles of my shoes scuffed over the stone floor. Candlelight flickered from each pillar and behind the altar, and the aroma of incense wafted around me. I pressed my finger to my upper lip to stop myself from sneezing.

I rarely stepped foot in churches. They didn't envelop me

with the sense of welcoming or homecoming that many people claimed it did for them. The eyes that stared down at me from the wooden and stone figures mounted on the walls made me uncomfortable.

La Madeleine was no different. For all the wealth of the archbishops and priests who governed this place, for all the devotion that poured forth during every service, it was just a building to me, the same people coming and going, the same sights and smells, if more vast and impressive, than many smaller chapels I'd seen in my sixty years of wandering.

I tracked down the church warden and requested to speak with Brother Godfrey, and not much later, his familiar scruffy face, mussed hair, and squinty eyes approached me.

"Madame Palon," he said. "It's been a long time. I didn't expect to see you again. After what happened, I worried you'd…"

I waved his worries aside. "You were able to save your books?"

His eyes lit up. "I was, yes."

"I wonder, is there somewhere we might speak? I was out walking this morning and saw something… something I fear might be related to what you confided to me on our journey here. About the cause of the trouble in Languedoc."

His bushy eyebrows climbed, and he invited me to sit with him on a low wooden bench along the back of the church, far from anyone currently at prayer and tucked away so our voices wouldn't carry. The wood creaked as I settled myself, and Godfrey joined me.

"It would be best to keep our conversation quiet," he said. "As yet, I've not been able to convince anyone of my theory, and I believe I've stirred up more scorn here than I did back in Lyon."

"I understand."

"Tell me, my child. What did you see?"

"A dark shape in the shadows of the woods with glowing red eyes and sharp teeth. It seemed to be reaching out for me. I ran and came straight here, realizing it must be this creature you talked of and knowing I must learn how to protect myself from it."

My feigned weakness tasted bitter, but by the concern in Godfrey's eyes, it was clear my act had swayed him.

He took my hand. "Prayer is your best defence. If you follow the true Church, you will be saved. It is only the heretics that are in danger here."

I swallowed my retort. "What of the summoners you mentioned? You said you saw them along your travels?"

He frowned, his brown eyes shifting as he stared into the shadows around the room, as though he expected someone to jump out of them. "A group of six nobles. The last I saw of them was outside Montpellier. Wealthy. Supposedly devout.

Cruel to their servants, preferring fear over respect from those they lead. And, as I mentioned before, a few priests among them, which concerns me greatly."

"You believe they might deal with demons to gain power?"

He scowled. "Fiends. Heathens. I wouldn't put it past them."

I considered what Emrick had said about the likelihood of a demon being able to end my life, but the same wouldn't hold true of the people who'd summoned it. If I could deal with them and find a way to send this demon back to the hell it came from, perhaps the fire driving the Crusade would die out before it consumed many more lives.

"What do you know of demons, Brother Godfrey?"

He pursed his lips and leaned back against the stone wall, stretching his legs out in front of him so his knees popped. "They come from a world beyond our own, cast down by God to fester and burn. They feed on the worst of humanity. Our fear, anger, lust, greed. They can only reach our world through powerful magic. A summoning. And they can only be cast back to the pit through the power of Christ."

I hoped that wasn't the case; otherwise, my mission had failed before it had begun.

"Most dangerous of all, they work through temptation. They'll tell you everything you want to hear until you're under their sway. They bring chaos in their wake, and those who fall prey to them are impervious to the call of reason or reality."

A bell tolled from within, and Godfrey rose to his feet to leave.

"Keep faith, madame. Pray. Avoid this evil."

"I will do what I can. I promise."

"May the blessings of God go with you."

He walked away, leaving me on the bench with my thoughts. If this beast was as powerful as Godfrey believed, someone needed to put it down before its darkness spread to cover more than the south of France.

I had to put my fear behind me, summon my courage along with my magic, and do my best to face this demon if no one else could.

Godfrey had said he'd last seen the summoners near Montpellier, and if they were accompanying the Crusaders, they were likely still there. It was too late in the day to begin the journey, but I would leave with the dawn and see where the route took me.

12

Katerina

Béziers, France - July 1209

BY THAT EVENING, word came to us that the Crusaders had reached Montpellier, holding there to give the army time to gather.

Their proximity, with their eyes fixed on Béziers, added urgency to the daunting task ahead of me.

"The priests are recommending their followers leave," I said to Jean the next morning as I set my water skin and some dried rations aside for my walk towards—but hopefully not into—the enemy's waiting hands. "Would you consider it?"

His gaze fell on his son's mop of brown hair, and he shook his head. "This is our home. These are our friends. They asked us to turn out the heretics to save ourselves, and I spat on their request. Now they tell us to leave? While our neighbours stay here to fend for themselves? We will hold our own."

While I admired his courage, I didn't share his optimism. Not if that demon remained among the soldiers, whispering words of fear and hate. But if I could stop it, distract it, send it away, perhaps reason would prevail among the men leading the army.

"I wish you luck in your travels, madame," Jean said, meeting my eye, his expression a mask of concern. "I understand you choosing to leave, but I don't know if going now, with those soldiers so close, is a wise decision."

I smiled. "Thank you for everything, Jean. God willing, I'll see you again in peaceful times."

The child tilted his head, requesting a kiss, and I gave him a peck on the cheek. Edith came into the room, wringing her hands, her swollen belly pressed against her dress. Her daughter clung to her leg.

I made my farewells to them all and started out. Dawn was only just breaking over the horizon, but Montpellier was two days away at a steady pace—one, if I didn't stop—and I wanted to make good distance while time allowed.

The tension that had hung in the air on my arrival had thickened into a choking fog. Gone were the merry faces wandering the streets. The only people out were those with no choice.

Everyone else was inside, no doubt praying or, I hoped, making plans for escape.

Soon, I left the city towards Montpellier.

Where possible, I stayed off the roads, doing my best to avoid the soldiers that were making camp along the river. Their intentions worried me. So many troops besieging the city would mean the bloodshed of too many innocents, especially with the mercenaries mixed in. Men that unprincipled and violent wouldn't care who they went after as long as they could indulge their bloodlust.

The desire came over me to wipe them out right here. A few strong bursts of fire to chase them back to Lyon.

But how long would it be before word spread that magic had been used outside Béziers? All it would do was paint a larger target on the city. So I gritted my teeth, clenched my fists into my skirt, and pressed on. The demon had to be my focus. Only with it gone could sanity return to the region and lives be saved, even if I had to give my own in return.

By midday, I had walked half of my expected route and so far seen no sign of nobles, priests, or demons. My feet ached, sweat pooled in the small of my back and under the seams around my wrists, but I plodded on, determination driving every step.

As I walked, I practiced with my fire, drawing on Emrick's impromptu lesson to improve my control over the flames that danced on my palms. His few words of advice had shaken loose some of the timber that had blocked me from a better understanding of my magic. I'd always been so quick to release it and wondered why it wouldn't obey my will. The simple act of holding on to it, directing it with my intention before sending it beyond my fingertips, had changed my view on everything—from how I manipulated my power to how I carried it within me.

The flame in my palm had become an extension of myself. My lifeblood turned to light.

But even as I prided myself on how far I'd come, I acknowledged how much of my power remained a mystery. I was out here with the aim of facing down a being able to twist the minds of thousands. How could I stand against it, as small and inferior as I was?

A tiny voice in the back of my mind tried to chase my doubts away, but they clung to me and squeezed out all other thoughts.

I was a fool to be out here. I would lose, possibly die, and for what? The world was doomed regardless.

My heart raced as fear overtook me, and only vaguely was I aware of how quickly the darkness had come over me, crushing out all hope and motivation.

Weak. Powerless. Alone. Why continue? Why bother taking another step when you know nothing will ever change?

The voice in my head twisted into a rasping whisper that bypassed my ears and settled directly in my soul.

Knots squeezed my stomach, my pulse raced faster, and I jumped as a priest stepped out from behind a tree less than ten paces ahead. His hands were clasped in front of him, and his eyes were filled with sorrow. The image of compassion and understanding. Of comfort and reassurance.

The hair on the back of my neck rose, and I drew to a stop.

The deep lines on his face and the stoop of his shoulders made him look older than I suspected he was. Thin brown hair flecked with grey was cut short to his head, his brown eyes were sunken, and his jowls wobbled with each breath.

"You seem troubled, my child." His voice was soft and deep, a sort of lulling flow that lured me closer to seek solace in his presence.

"I'm searching for a group of people," I said. "I don't suppose you've seen them on your travels along this road? Nobles, mostly, I believe. Perhaps a few of your brothers among them."

He tilted his head, but the rest of him remained eerily still. "Why do you seek these people? You, a lost, wandering lamb. You don't fear they would harm you? Ruin your body, corrupt your soul?"

His words crawled down my spine, caused my heart to rattle against my ribs and my breath to catch. My trembling legs threatened to give out and send me sprawling across the earth.

What power was this that he could instill such deep terror in my bones with a few words? Godfrey had said priests were among the summoners. Was this one of them? If so, what did I have to fear from him? Yet in this moment, my desire to run was greater than my will to fight.

An infernal touch was all over this man.

"I have no intention of running in without thought," I said, "but if I can prevent these people from harming others, I will. If you've seen them and know where they are, I would appreciate you pointing me in their direction."

The priest took a step forward, and suddenly he was right in front of me, as though his long legs had eaten the ground between us. The air prickled my skin, tense with energy, and my mouth went dry.

"You can't stop them, my dear. You know you can't. You don't have what it takes." His breath brushed across my cheek, stale and foul.

Now that he stood so close, I noticed the greying pallor of his wrinkled face. His lips were bloodless, almost blue, and the dips of his eyes were a deep red.

As soon as he stopped talking, I realized the smell of decay wasn't limited to his breath. It wafted off his clothes, his skin. Although he was a living, breathing man, he may as well have been decomposing in front of me.

And as that detail sank in, my stomach dropped into the soles of my boots. This priest wasn't only touched by the infernal—he *was* the infernal.

A small smile stretched his mouth wide. "There's that healthy fear, my child." He closed his eyes and inhaled, as though I presented the sweetest bouquet. "Allow me to take it from you. I can offer what no one else can—an end to your fears. No more worries, no more nightmares. And oh, how I sense your nightmares. How long have they chased you through the darkness? Longer than most people would guess, I suspect."

He licked his lips, and when he opened his eyes, they were a shocking red that should have struck terror in my heart. But there was no terror—only a strange, uncomfortable numbness.

I'd come here looking for a demon, and he had found me unprepared.

"You've been driving the hate against the heretics," I said.

"Such an easy focus for people who fear losing their power more than their souls."

"Who are you?"

"I am Shogaur, a demon of fear. Many deem me a monster, but what kind of monster offers such peace of mind?" He reached a green-tinged hand towards my face and brushed my hair behind my ear. At the contact, sharp pain lanced through my skull, and I recoiled from his touch even as his eyes brightened. "I sense such power in you. Untapped. Unexplored. Delicious. We could make such a pairing, *Katerina.*"

My name slithered over his tongue, causing the chill in my bones to deepen.

Pressure built in my head, cold fingers sliding under my scalp and squeezing my skull. Or pressing out? Both at once. I closed my eyes and took another step back, but Shogaur followed, his hands on my shoulders, his red eyes working to catch mine.

"For months, I've searched for someone with your strength. Someone who could carry me longer than a few days at a time. Let me in, Katerina. You see how this host withers away. I need your power to help me in my mission to remove the fear from this world."

I laughed, though it came with an effort. "Yes, I'm certain that's your goal. How magnanimous of you."

He grinned, and a cockroach skittered over his teeth. "In order to remove it, one must first unleash it. A few well-placed words is more than enough to do the trick. Very low effort for great reward—for everyone involved."

I summoned fire into my palm and rested it against his chest. "You'll never involve me."

The heat pushed him back with a hiss, and his eyes flared as he came for me again. "I'm sorry, my dear. I didn't realize you thought you had a choice."

His hand came up to strike me, but I was ready for it and

ducked beneath his arm, hurling another fireball into his face. It struck his cheek with a sizzle, and my vision wavered as a creature tore itself out of the priest. The old man collapsed to the ground, and the demon itself remained standing.

In his true form, he appeared almost human, though no one would confuse him with one. He towered over me by at least a head, his skin as grey and slick as the decomposing corpse he'd just vacated. His narrow frame was draped in black cloth like a shroud, but more terrifying than the rest of him were the shining, pointed teeth in his wide grin, as sharp as the talons that extended from his long, grey fingers.

He cried out as he flew at me, his arms wrapping around my middle to take me to the ground.

As Shogaur attempted to dominate me, I reversed the heat of my magic and rested my iced palms on the earth. Frost spread quickly, thickened to ice, and wrapped around his ankles. He started, looked down, and I took the opening to scurry clear of him. He tried to stand, but the ice held him fast.

My confidence soared. All I needed now was his blood before I recited the words Emrick had taught me to send him back to the infernal realms.

In the few moments I had while he concentrated on freeing himself, I drew the knife from the pocket of my apron and approached him, ready to set the blade against his throat. But as I knelt, he laughed and swung his arm, catching me on the side of the face. He kicked his way out of the ice and pinned me down, one hand on my throat, the other holding my wrist, slamming my hand against the rocky soil until I released the blade.

The pressure in my head swelled as he tried once more to crawl inside, and I flailed against him, determined to keep him out. He slipped deeper, and suddenly I was staring at the world from my position beneath him but also seeing my face below, trapped between the two as he fought to take over my mind.

I tried to push him back, but he was too strong. A master of his skills, while I was barely an apprentice.

Desperate, I set my hand on the side of his face and pumped as much fire as I could into my palm. The reek of charred flesh filled my nose, but I didn't stop, channelling more and more power into my fingers. He bared his teeth and tried to work through the pain, but his hold on my wrist weakened, and I scrabbled in the leaves for the hilt of my knife. As soon as my fingers wrapped around it, I drove it into the side of his neck.

He cried out and flew back. I jumped to my feet, aching and covered in sweat. Before I could catch my breath to begin the incantation, Shogaur was out of sight, though his touch on my mind remained.

I bent over and heaved.

Emrick was right. I wasn't ready to face this monster. But now that he'd targeted me as his next host, what choice did I have but to keep tracking him?

With him injured and lacking human form, I would never get a better opportunity to overpower him than right now.

My legs shook, my heart raced, but my need to stop him drove me onwards. Shogaur might underestimate me, but let him. I would show him what my teachers had failed to appreciate.

I did not give up easily.

13

Katerina

Béziers, France - July 1209

Y HEAD, MY throat, my shoulders throbbed as I pushed through the trees, following the blood trail Shogaur had left behind in his speedy flight.

Everywhere the demon had touched me ached, as though his hands had worked their magic to set a permanent chill in my bones. My body was healing, but his power had been greater than any I'd faced before. I was worn out, sore, and very aware of my ineptitude in the face of this fight. If there were a way to contact Emrick to get more advice, I might have been tempted to try, but he would only warn me away again, and I still wouldn't listen.

Not when I stood a chance of hunting the demon while he was weak enough for me to grab the upper hand. All the better if it meant putting an end to this Crusade and saving the people who had taken me in and shown such kindness.

I hadn't known the Artois family long, but everything about their lives reminded me of what I had lost. The way Janine's arms wrapped around my leg when I came into a room was an experience I'd never had with my son, who hadn't even learned to walk by the time he was taken from me. If I could spare anyone else that pain, it was worth some discomfort on my part.

The blood trail led me off the road for a good while, leading straight to a small, crumbling chapel hidden deep in the woods. Most of the roof was gone, open to the elements, and through the gap, I spotted a flicker of firelight coming from within.

Doubting Shogaur would have need of a fire, I drew my magic inwards so the flames were no longer visible around my gloves and stepped quietly forward. Voices carried on the wind, a weave of well-spoken French that suggested the people speaking not only hailed from north of here but came from wealthier society. A tinkling laugh spilled through a deep guffaw. Men and women, then.

The summoners?

I searched the area for Shogaur, but there was no sign of him and the stink of sulphur had faded. Was he hiding inside the chapel with the people who'd brought him to this plane?

Fear held me bound. Going up against the demon again would be challenge enough, but to face him and the magic users who'd summoned him?

But who could I call on for help? No, I wasn't ready to go up against them, but the whole country might burn if I waited until I was.

Drawing in a deep breath, doing my best to wrangle my terror and bury it under my need to fight back this evil, I took another few steps forward, hoping to catch a glimpse of the people within before they noticed me.

I half-expected them to appear as twisted and corrupt as their minds obviously were to be sending demons against innocents to maintain their power. But when I peered around the corner, I was surprised to see just how mundane they were. Four men and two women, two priests and four nobles, sat around the fire, enclosed within a chalk circle marked with protective runes. Aside from their colourful wools and expensive silks, I might have passed any of them on the street and not given them a second glance.

Yet they had done the unthinkable and opened the barrier between realms to wreak havoc on the world. Why? Because these Good Christians spoke of humility and equality? Because they spurned the Catholic priests for hoarding wealth that could be put to better use?

These bastards held positions of leadership, positions of trust, and had turned against the people who relied on them.

Waves of red blurred my vision as anger sparked like fire in my blood.

Shogaur was nowhere to be seen among them. I cursed my bad luck that I had likely missed my chance to attack his weakened form, but I refused to give up the opportunity to deal with those who had brought him here.

With my magic simmering below the surface of my skin, not visible but ready to be called, I stepped into the open doorway and revealed myself to the group within.

I kept my mind open, willing to give them a chance to explain the markings on the floor, to swear they weren't the people who had summoned Shogaur, but the man in front, one of the nobles, had no interest in explanations as he spoke an incantation that created a spell circle in the air in front of him.

The circle brightened into a glow, then burst outwards in a rush of air that nearly forced me off my feet.

A woman behind him followed up the spell by hurling a knife at me. The blade lodged in my side, and I hunched over it, both hands wrapped around the hilt as I struggled to breathe through the pain.

I should have come in hotter, ready for them to attack.

A mistake I would not make again.

Clenching my teeth, I jerked the knife free and threw it to

the ground behind me. As I straightened, my flesh tugged and pulled, knitting itself together, and gasps and shouts sounded from inside as they backed away from me.

"Demon!" one of the priests shouted, crossing himself.

A laugh escaped me. "Are you afraid because of what you believe me to be, or because you weren't the one to bring me here?"

I drew fire into my palms and this time let it fly, first at the woman who'd thrown the knife, then at the man who'd cast the spell. The woman leapt out of the way, and the fireball hit the other woman standing behind her. Her skirts caught, and the fire spread, catching the dried wood of the broken bench beneath her.

The two priests closed in on me, muttering Latin phrases under their breath. I canted my head to the side and watched them. "Are you trying to send me back to the dark pit, Fathers? I'm afraid you'll be disappointed. I'm as human are you are."

The horror in their eyes was almost satisfying as I threw two more fireballs their way.

Somewhere in the back of my mind, a little voice nagged at me that I was working against what my parents would have wanted. By going after these magic users instead of the demon, I was attacking those weaker than myself.

The reek of charred flesh and burning cloth, the empty eyes of the spellcaster who lay dead on the floor as the fire raged on, turned my stomach and shattered my heart, but what would it mean if this group had been left to summon more demons? These people had known what they were doing when they'd brought Shogaur from the depths. In ridding the world of these six, how many thousands would I save?

"You sought to preserve your power by attacking those with less," I said. "Instead of using your influence to help those in need, you wielded it to destroy them."

The remaining woman, wisely hiding behind the last-standing man, crossed her arms. "These heretics are far from innocent, demon. They spread like a sickness, bending others to their beliefs, coming for our wealth, our positions. Do you condemn them as well? Why should we not call upon every resource at our disposal? Shogaur promises success, glory, everything beyond our wildest dreams."

"You trust the word of a demon?"

They might have been skilled summoners, but intelligence seemed to be spread thinly among them.

"He is under our control," the man said. He held a knife in his hand, but unlike the woman appeared hesitant to throw it. He had to know there was no point; I would simply use it against him. "We say when he returns to hell. We say when he ceases his task. While he remains with us, we have the power."

I thought of my conversation with Shogaur, remembered his talk of whispers and manipulations, the voice in my head trying to convince me I was worthless.

"And without him, you're nothing, aren't you? For all your titles and wealth, you are insignificant scabs on the face of this earth. You'll never achieve anything on your own."

The waver in his gaze told me I'd guessed correctly. Shogaur was working his influence on them as much as he was on the priests that had denounced the heretics. Little whispers to shake their confidence and force them to hand their control into his hands. I had to give the demon credit for knowing his craft so well.

"It ends here," I said. "I can absorb my fire if you promise to reverse the ritual and send Shogaur back where he belongs. End this death and destruction."

The man barked a laughed. "You think sending him back will stop what's begun? Every day, more soldiers pour into Languedoc, encouraged by the Pope himself, rallying behind Amalric, who is biting at the bit to attack. That man is hungry to spill first blood. To prove his worth before God."

My stomach tightened. Although I didn't want to believe him, his words rang true. Shogaur wasn't forcing people into their fears; he was drawing out what already existed, which meant the Papal Bull would remain in effect even if the demon who'd influenced its signing disappeared, and the Papal legate would continue his march on Béziers. I would need to track down Amalric and attempt to talk him out of this crusade, a task that might prove impossible. Easier, perhaps, to return to the city and try again to convince Jean and his family to leave before the soldiers marched. But at least without Shogaur's influence, the possibility existed that this fabricated fear would no longer spread. Tempers would fade, reason would inject itself back into the minds of the common men and women, and the priests could return to preaching faith rather than turning neighbours against each other.

"So you refuse?" I asked, giving these people one last chance to save their lives.

"We have nothing to refuse," the man said. "You'll be the one to die today."

He threw his knife, aimed at my heart, but I side-stepped the blade and returned his volley with one of my own. Screams filled the chapel as the fire caught both him and the woman behind him. A second fireball caught the reeds bunched on the floor in the corner. The fire spread quickly, eating the dry wood of the benches and the abandoned altar. I fed more into it, wanting to show them mercy with a quick death—the least I could offer.

The stench in the air coated the back of my throat, and bile bubbled up to spill between my lips. I bent over and heaved the contents of my empty stomach onto the ground, filled with horror at what I'd done now that it was over.

Behind me, the fire raged as the dead trees that had fallen

through the open roof caught flame, and before long the entire chapel was consumed in an inferno that drew sweat from my pores and singed the tips of my hair.

I staggered away before I was swept up myself, and with every step came more contractions of my stomach.

It didn't matter that they'd brought forth the demon that had a hand in threatening tens of thousands of lives—I had just killed six people.

My parents had always talked about doing whatever was necessary to maintain the balance between magical and mundane, but was this what they meant? How would they justify taking these lives? Would they see a difference between going after the wyverns and harpies that threatened our secret and what these humans had done, or would they agree I'd made the best decision?

I would never know the answer, but I did know I never wanted to experience this pain again. Driving my magic through Shogaur's heart was something I would do with pleasure and no guilt, but never again would I take a human life if I could avoid it. I swore it.

Gradually, my churning stomach settled, and I turned away from the fire—only to find myself facing the raised swords of eight Crusaders.

My heart leapt into my throat as one of them sheathed their weapon and stepped forward. I waited for him to speak, blood rushing so loudly in my ears I doubted I'd hear whatever he said.

But he didn't say anything as he raised a gauntleted hand and swung the back of it at my face. A burst of pain rattled my skull and shot across my cheekbone, and the ground came up to meet me. He pressed a heavy knee into my lower back and bound my hands behind me.

"So be it," he whispered in my ear. "You should have let me take you, Katerina."

14

Katerina

France - July 1209

MY CELL WAS dark and cold and reeked of blood and human waste.

I hadn't been the only prisoner over my two-day stint in this hole, but I was the only one remaining. The screams of the others had kept me awake and turned my already frozen bones to ice. I'd tried to escape so I could help them, but my attempts to use my fire on the metal bars or stone walls had done nothing more than drain my energy.

On the journey here, as the soldier-Shogaur dragged me by my hair and his fellows tried to torture me into confessing my heresy, I'd scared them with my rapid healing. Broken fingers had repaired themselves within hours, bruises and lacerations had disappeared within minutes.

Accusations of sorcery echoed around me, but they had no idea how little sorcery had to do with it.

Unfortunately, while I was saved any extended discomfort, I wasn't spared the agony of the initial injuries, and the echo of what they'd done remained long after the marks were gone. The joints in my hands throbbed, my knees, ankles, hips screamed with every movement.

Once the soldiers realized they couldn't cause me any permanent damage—and once Shogaur had enjoyed his fill of my torment—they'd abandoned me in this cell. I was certain they weren't finished with me, but the waiting was as much a torture as their hands-on care.

I tugged my shift over my feet. The dun wool was stained with blood and muck and reeked of mould, and I suspected it had covered the bodies of more than one woman who'd walked these dripping halls. My clothes had been burned in front of me, along with the food Edith had so kindly prepared, and my knife had been confiscated by one of the soldiers and used to open my arm from elbow to palm just so they could watch the splayed flesh seal itself. When my runed gloves had refused to burn, they'd confiscated those as well, the loss of which hurt more than anything else. All they'd left me with was this threadbare shift and a thin rope belt around my waist.

I was very strongly reconsidering my vow of not killing any more humans.

At present, the only thoughts keeping me going were those of vengeance, and I comforted myself with the idea that the screams bounding off these stone walls came from my captors instead of my fellow captives.

But these soldiers weren't in their right minds. They had been influenced by a demon of fear, and they were acting on primal instincts to defend themselves from what they perceived to be a threat. The heretics they hunted went against everything they had been raised to believe, and if they allowed the Good Christians to live, they would be forced to question their values, their religion, their entire outlook on life.

Nothing I said would pull these men back now that they'd begun. Not with the Pope behind them and the Papal legate driving them on.

I'd been naïve to think I could. Stopping the demon and his summoners was only half the battle, and even there I'd failed.

And now I faced whatever future awaited me. If the opportunity presented to escape, I would take it, but Shogaur knew what I was and had seen what—or what little—I was capable of. He would stand in my way, and I wouldn't be able to best him.

With no way of reaching out to Emrick, my only options were to accept my fate or figure out my own solution. In the time I had left, I pushed through the stiffness in my limbs, rose to my feet, and summoned my magic. It began as a tickle around my heart that spread down my arms and into my fingers, warming me despite the dampness in the room. Once my power simmered beneath my skin, I pushed it to the surface, sending flames over my palms. The light flickered off the dark, slick walls, and I pointedly ignored the red stains spattered across the filthy straw and grey stone to focus on the wall outside the cell.

I couldn't burn my way out, but if I could heat the bars, perhaps I could bend them enough to push through. Not without a great deal of pain, but my hands would heal and I would be free.

"It's good that you enjoy playing with fire, Katerina."

The red-eyed soldier came into view and graced me with a wide smile.

I hadn't heard his footsteps coming down the stairs, but now that he stood in front of me, his rotting odor slunk up my nostrils and coated the back of my throat. It had to be strong if it overpowered the other repulsive scents of my accommodations.

Unlike the decaying priest, this man had been in his prime when Shogaur took over his body. Strong muscles, a close-cropped black beard, and large eyes; a handsome exterior to hide the evil within. Not unusual in this world, but rarely so literal.

"I suggest you keep your distance," I said. "Unless you enjoyed being caught in my flame."

I flicked a fireball through the bars, but he side-stepped the attack and watched with a bland expression as it struck the wall and fizzled out.

He turned back to face me. "Not today, I'm afraid. Nor ever again. One way or another, your games end here."

I frowned, not catching his meaning until three soldiers with glazed eyes marched down the steps to stop alongside him.

"Why are you listening to him?" I asked. "Are you so eager to commit murder that you take orders from a demon?"

Shogaur grinned. "They see nothing, sorceress. These soldiers are my pets, not the Abbot's, and they only know what I want them to know, which is nightmare and pain." He stepped closer to the bars. "That doesn't have to be you. I present you with a choice, Katerina." The demon's voice slid through my ears, the syllables of my name tripping over his tongue like a savoured delicacy. "Allow me into your mind, let me take you away from this place so we can work together to bring the world to its knees, or you burn. Right now."

My mouth went dry. "Those aren't options, Shogaur. Two versions of hell is not a choice."

He laughed. "My dear, you have no concept of hell. Your mortal mind cannot comprehend the agony and depravity that await me should I return. So I will not return. These bodies I inhabit last so little time. Without magic in their blood, they wither and decay." He reached out his hand, and I noted the blackened nail beds. "Your power, however, would ensure my continuation for years. Decades. Perhaps longer."

He inhaled slowly, nostrils flaring, and I was again reminded of someone scenting flowers offered by a lover.

My bones quaked with horror and disgust.

"I will never host you. Burn me, torture me, kill me if you can, but my mind will remain my own."

Shogaur bared his teeth, and my stomach twisted at the sight of maggots writhing in the pockets of his mouth. "I win either way. Your terror and pain as the fire devours you will fuel my appetite for weeks. Your screams will satisfy me for years."

I made no boastful claims about holding those screams back or not being afraid to die. He would know the latter was untrue, and the former… well, the summoners had shown me what immolation could do to a person.

My heart raced despite my best efforts to stay calm, and Shogaur's smile widened.

"Men, bring her to the pyre. I'm in need of a feast."

One of the soldiers opened the door, and I darted for the opening as soon as he stepped back. Flames licked over my hands as I shoved a second soldier out of the way, but footsteps echoed on the stone, and even as the man I'd shoved hissed at the contact with my scorching fingers, three more soldiers appeared on the stairs with another dozen standing at the top. One of the soldiers gripped the arm of a young woman. I didn't know her, but I didn't have to. The terror in her eyes, her shift that matched mine, and the bruise on her cheek told me she was another victim of Shogaur's power and humanity's drive for self-preservation.

"I should mention you have a third choice," the demon hissed in my ear.

Again, I felt the tendrils of his influence crawling into my head, and I imagined the trap around my mind as Emrick had taught me, sealing it shut and leaving no room for Shogaur to get in.

"You could burn your way free," he said. "Unleash your fire and destroy the building. Roast these soldiers, that young woman, all the other people we have upstairs or caged down here. What are their lives compared to your liberty?"

His dark chuckle told me he'd seen my reaction after killing the summoners. He knew I couldn't—wouldn't—do it. Not to the soldiers, but especially not to this innocent woman caught in a lethal net thanks to one small group's ambitions.

While a chance remained, however small, that she might survive and go home to her family, how could I take that from her?

My shoulders slumped as I pulled my magic into myself,

and the soldiers grabbed my arms. The one I'd burned struck me a backhanded blow across the face, and I spat blood onto the manky straw at my feet.

Their grip on my arms was strong, and my toes scrambled to find purchase to walk on my own as they hauled me up the stairs.

As I climbed, the stench of blood grew stronger, as did the odor of pitch and pine that curdled on my tongue. After three days in almost total darkness, the sunlight streaming through the windows when we reached the top made me turn away. Sunset, I guessed, based on the red-orange glow that spilled across the floor. So much like the fire to come.

Once my eyes adjusted, I took in the scene around me, desperate to find my way out. We were in some kind of church, though I doubted it was any consecrated building based on who led these soldiers. The interior was empty, stripped of anything that might benefit me if I got my hands on it. Nothing but worn-down stone and splashes of blood. By the screams that followed me, I guessed there were other passages down to the depths where more supposed heretics were undergoing their *purification*.

I wished I could do more to help, but unless I found my way out, they were as trapped as I was.

The soldiers jerked me forward, leading me towards the set of double doors and a courtyard outside. In the seconds left to me before we passed outdoors, I scrambled to come up with a plan. As soon as I had space, I would reverse my fire, summon my ice, and force my guards to release me. Then I would take advantage of their surprise and run. They would give chase, but a few well-aimed fireballs would hold them back.

Once I was free, I would track down the Abbot of Citeaux, the Papal legate leading these Crusaders on their mission, and warn him of Shogaur's influence. Surely a devoted, religious man would see the danger a demon posed. He wasn't likely to turn his back on his Crusade, but maybe I could give the people of Béziers time to escape.

Either way, I would not let Shogaur win.

I hung on to my plan right up to the point when I was pulled into the courtyard and saw how prepared the demon was. Dozens of Crusaders stood around a platform where a stake had been anchored. There was no way I'd be able to take three steps without someone blocking my path. I could have fought through, was nearly driven to do it out of the terror hugging my insides, but Shogaur had been ready for that possibility as well. Between every few guards stood a struggling innocent. Men and women, children no older than ten. All of them scared, confused, as desperate to escape as I was.

Would I be doing them a favour by incinerating them? By the look of some of them, probably, but doing so would mean more weight on my shoulders, more burden to add to the others I already carried. Perhaps it was selfish of me, but I couldn't do it.

Which meant I was locked within the walls of my conscience, forced to stare down Shogaur's ultimatum. Live with a demon invading my mind or possible death.

Hopeful death.

Definite agony.

My throat closed on a sob, and I upbraided myself for my cowardice. I'd told Emrick I was willing to die if it meant stopping this demon. Letting Shogaur take me over was out of the question, and if keeping him out meant my death, so be it. I would use my final moments to take him down with me.

Legs trembling, too aware of my chance of success shrinking, I allowed the soldiers to push me up the steps to the wooden stake.

"Are you sure you want to miss the rest of the party?" Shogaur asked. He stood before me, too far for me to reach out and grab him but close enough for me to see the mottling of his skin as it leached up from under his surcoat. "I understand Abbot Amalric intends to carry out some tasty plans for your friends in Béziers tomorrow."

I spared a thought for Jean, Edith, and their children. Such kindness, such goodness. But they were Catholic. Surely, at the very least, the Abbot would spare those who followed his precious faith.

For the others, the best I could do was try to prevent the situation from worsening. Human crusades could only last so long before interest and funding waned. Without demonic influence, I prayed to *my* gods that reason returned soon.

"Nothing you say will change my mind," I said. "You will never use me."

"A pity, my dear. But I will enjoy this all the same."

The soldiers bound my arms behind the stake, tying my wrists so tightly I lost all feeling in my fingers, and secured more rope around my waist to keep me in place. Then they heaped straw around the base of where I stood, splashing both straw and my shift in oil to help the fire burn hotter.

My heart raced so quickly I couldn't catch my breath, but I gritted my teeth and refused to show the fear Shogaur was syphoning off me. I hated that I was giving him that much, but it was all he'd get.

Two of the soldiers knelt beside me and struck their flints into the kindling. With every strike, every spark, my desperation surged. I summoned my magic and tried to ignite the rope binding my wrists, but the fibres refused to light. Pain scored my skin, and though I did my best to ignore it, I couldn't find the strength to pump more heat into my hands. I'd used so much magic in the past couple of days my reserves had yet to recover. If I wanted to stop Shogaur, I would need to be smart with whatever I had left.

Smoke drifted up from the lit straw, and the flames spread slowly, tickling my toes with their painful tongues, teasing the torment to come. As it reached the oil, the fire spat, and the soldiers hurried away to avoid being caught in the shooting spray. I was left to suffer the horror of watching the fire consume the kindling, sweep over the straw, caress the hem of my shift.

The wool caught, and the fire devoured the oil-touched cloth like a starving beast.

I tugged at the bindings around my wrists, jerked so hard the joints popped out of place, but the knots were so tight I gained no traction.

The flames kissed my bare feet, my shins, and all the while, Shogaur stared on, his sick grin firmly in place, his eyes filled with eagerness and greed. The two soldiers, apparently satisfied with their task, left the platform to join the others. The innocents that had stayed my hand were forced to stand and watch, despair in their eyes as they stared into their likely future.

The eyes of the soldiers, however, were as empty as the ones who had taken me from my cell, all of them pinned under Shogaur's influence, nothing of their own minds left.

Smoke billowed around me, filling the air and my lungs with its thickness, and I clenched my teeth until a sharp pain shot through my jaw.

A scream escaped my throat through my closed lips, and

I sucked in a breath to stop more from following, though the intake of smoke threw me into a coughing fit.

Pain spread over my knees, my thighs, and soon enough, I wasn't able to hold back the whimpers as my flesh sizzled.

Shogaur closed his eyes, his expression turning blissful. He didn't need to watch me suffer. He picked up every emotion as it swept over me, savouring my terror. My anger, too, no doubt. My regret.

But while his eyes were closed, I fought through the cloudiness of my tortured body and summoned my fire. Against the agony at my feet, I no longer noticed the pain in my wrists as the flames heated the rope, crept over my hands and up my arms. The more power I channelled, the more the fire at my feet swept outwards, pushed back by the magical flames I'd created. The pain didn't lessen but neither did it spread, and my relief was enough to clear my head and let me send my magic outwards. The fire crept through the straw and along the platform until it reached Shogaur's boots.

He opened his eyes in surprise and staggered back, but not before I reversed the flow of my magic. Frost doused the fire on my hands and followed the path of the flame, most of the magic still hidden from the eyes of the people on the ground by the thick clouds of smoke. As it passed over my legs, hugging my flesh, the sweetness of reprieve swept over me, along with the hope that I might find my way out after all.

The temptation was strong to douse the fire around me before anything else, but as my strength waned and my vision blurred, I forced myself to concentrate on the more important goal. With another surge of magic, the ice devoured the flames creeping up Shogaur's legs and hardened, thickened, rooting him to the platform.

He struggled to free himself, but I had him, and despite my exhaustion and wavering consciousness, I couldn't help but grin.

Although everywhere the ice touched, the fire petered out, everywhere else it blazed so hot and fast that sweat broke out along my spine and my hairline even as goosebumps formed on my arms. I tried to summon a layer of frost to protect me from the fire licking at my back, but my energy was draining too quickly, and my hold on Shogaur's ice cage was slipping.

With a low cry to brace myself, I released the magic covering me and directed it towards Shogaur. I needed him out of his host, and I needed his blood. Only then could I send him back to the dark pit where he belonged.

With the fire closing in on me again, it was all I could do to hold back my screams. I suspected in mere moments I would lose that fight, the searing heat already pressing into my skin, creating cold-hot sensations that bit straight into muscle and bone. I prayed I'd be able to stay conscious until I'd done my duty… and after that, I prayed the rest would be quick.

Tears streamed down my cheeks, evaporating as quickly as they fell, and my breathing grew laboured, my breaths coming in rasping gasps as the smoke choked me.

Seconds. I had seconds to make a difference.

Pushing more magic through my struggling system, I wrapped more ice around the demon and wished I had my father's ability to summon lightning as well as fire. Shogaur fought against me, struggling to lift his feet out of the ice, to throw himself off the platform to safety, but I pumped more magic, thickening the prison around him.

As soon as he was encased, his lips blue, his beard white with frost, I reversed my magic again and pushed my fire along the path of the ice. Harder and faster, channelling more magic than I'd ever used at once.

Gasps and screams echoed beyond my own as the victims of the Crusade watched the events with growing panic, but the soldiers didn't react at all, locked in place by Shogaur's hold on them.

Until they weren't. As one, they slit the throats of the heretics and charged the platform, coming straight for me—dozens of men with armour and swords, ready to cut me to pieces to save their demon lord.

I felt the pull of both magic and strength pouring out of me. My vision grew spotty, my breath little more than a whistling wheeze, and the pain, oh gods the pain. It blocked out all thought except for the single line of words repeating through my head.

Flames wrapped around Shogaur, and in a burst of smoke, he launched himself from his host.

With the moments remaining to me, I was ready for him with a spear of ice that shot up from the platform and speared him in the stomach. His cry blocked out mine, but I couldn't hold back any longer from screaming out the agony of my flesh blistering, peeling, cooking where I stood roped to this stake. My hands were lost in the flames, all sensation of fingers and joints gone. Nothing but pain and a prayer for an end.

But Shogaur was still here, and he was fleeing as his soldiers closed in. A sword pierced my side, but I pitched my screams into the words Emrick had taught me to send the demon back to the infernal realms and felt the tug in my soul as my flagging magic reached out to grab him. Shogaur jerked to a halt as though a tether had wrapped around his chest, and I screamed louder, pouring all my desperation and determination into each strained syllable.

Another sword lodged in my shoulder; a third swiped into my side.

The world was growing darker, awareness seeping out with my sweat and blood, but I wasn't finished yet. I had to stay awake—alive—for a few more heartbeats.

My tongue swelled, too dry in my mouth and finding no

moisture in the smoke-clogged, fire-consumed air. The flames licked higher, caught my hair, and blackness crept in on me.

I choked on the next words as my body gave out.

It was over. I had failed.

My first and only attempt to redeem myself in the eyes of my dead family, and I had let them down again.

Yet my last thought wasn't for them but for Emrick. I regretted that I never had a chance to thank him for all he'd done and that I'd never get a chance to see him again. I prayed he would speak to Death on my behalf and let it take me.

15

Emrick

France - 1209

I SHOULD HAVE let Katerina die.

It would have been the compassionate choice. Perhaps for both of us. I would have saved another sliver of my soul and been free to return to the emptiness of my servitude. She would no longer suffer the pain of being without her family.

But I couldn't.

By the time I'd realized her predicament, she'd already suffered and healed from their torture, and I'd watched her in that cell, wavering on if and when and how I would step in to help.

She had made her decision knowing the consequences.

When I'd made my deal with Death, I had vowed to leave the lives of those on the earthly realm to their fates or risk becoming nothing more than a shade. Already I felt myself changing. Nothing anyone would notice, but some of my oldest, most treasured memories had begun to blur, the moments of my past that anchored me to who I was slipping out of reach. What else was I willing to give up?

Yet as I watched Kate fight to her last breath, transforming her pain into an attack against the demon that had begun this latest bloody streak in human history, I'd felt tension on the tether that bound us.

It had pulled so hard, I was sure it would snap. Her body was almost too far gone to heal. The soldiers had added their damage to what the flames had done, and in another few heartbeats, she would be lost to me.

Panic at having her ripped away forced me into action. The moment Kate's burned, sword-ravaged body sagged against the wooden stake, I stepped out of the afterlife into the flames. With a slice of my knife through the ropes that bound her, she collapsed into my arms, her weight so light, her shape so delicate.

My heart raced at the feel of her body cradled against mine, no sign in her that I'd made it in time except for the faintest pulse of the bond between us.

I made to step back through the mist to take her to

safety, but the sight of Shogaur snared in her unfinished spell compelled me to stop.

I knew I should keep walking. While I could justify saving Kate as she no longer held a place in the mortal world, the demon and its effects were well beyond my purview. But Kate had come so far, fought so hard, and I couldn't bring myself to let her efforts be in vain.

So I finished the words and experienced two uncomfortable jerks—one jerk a fragment of myself being wrenched from me, another memory gone perhaps, the other an effect of the fabric of the universe shifting as the barrier between realms split. A hole opened in the earth beneath Shogaur, and some unseen force dragged him down. He screamed and clawed at the ground, desperate to find purchase but not strong enough to counter the pull of his home. Then he was gone, the hole in the earth was gone, and the courtyard was silent except for the crackling flames.

Whether the soldiers would remember anything of what happened once they snapped out of his spell was none of my concern. My priority was the life I carried with me, the woman whose heart raced in time with my own, who was already beginning to heal—though given the state of her, I doubted the process of returning to her immortalized state would be quick or painless.

At the thought, another pang of uncertainty hit me.

Had I made a mistake in rescuing her?

I was too selfish to turn back. The thought of having that tether snap threatened to break something in me—my sanity or my heart, I wasn't sure. Probably both.

Holding her gently but securely, I stepped out of this world and into the next, needing to get her to safety and, curse my fate, ensure she survived to waken again.

16

Katerina

Darkness - Unknown

WHEN THE WORLD returned to me, so did the pain, and it wouldn't stop. I screamed and thrashed, my arms free from the ropes that bound them until suddenly they weren't, strapped down at my sides. Unable to move more than a few inches, I threw my head back and kicked my legs until those were bound as well, but nothing eased the sensation of every inch of my body being eaten, flayed, burned… everything at once.

Why wasn't I dead?

I'd accepted my fate despite my failure.

Oh gods, was this my punishment? My people didn't believe

in conscious life after death but what if we'd been wrong? What if my mistakes had led to this moment, and now there was no escape? An eternity of agony.

Beyond my screams and the roar of flames in my ears, a murmur of voices reached me, and although I couldn't make out a single word, the gentle intonation of one was familiar. At times, I thought it might be Shep. In occasional moments of wishful thinking, I imagined it was Rowan. That wherever I was, my son was grown and watching over me.

Sometimes the thought brought me comfort. The rest of the time, it broke me that I couldn't reach out and hold him.

Every once in a while, however, I was aware of something other than the mindless, endless, all-consuming pain. Something cool. Fingers sweeping my cheek. As soon as it was there, it was gone, buried under waves of flame that kissed my skin with a barbed tongue.

I prayed for the death I'd sworn was so close but, with the passing of time, felt farther away.

Eventually, I gave up on wishing and gave myself over to this new hell.

17

Emrick

Florence, Italy - August 1209

I PACED KATE'S room as I'd done every day for two weeks, unable to stop or leave.

Every day, as I watched her scream and try to escape her brutal natural healing, I questioned if I'd made the right decision. How would she come out of this the same person as before? She had endured so much already, and I had added to her suffering.

Would I be the one to suffer the greater agony if she refused to forgive me for stepping in? If she never looked at me again with that open, inviting expression? That smile she'd only graced me with a handful of times that I longed to see more of?

My breath caught at the idea that I might have lost her by saving her.

I scrubbed my hands over my face. It was too late for regrets. All I could do now was help her through this. I'd had to tie her down with soft cotton strips so she didn't tear her delicate, healing skin. Her hair was already growing back, the seeping welts fading as her flesh regrew. At this rate, it would take weeks if not months for a full physical recovery. Not even the bond between us could hasten the process more than that.

The door creaked open, and I looked up to see the familiar face of my only friend as he stepped into the room. He leaned against the wall and crossed his arms.

Adrian had lived long past his Roman heritage and name, though he kept his military bearing and physique, some-thing impossible not to notice in the close quarters of Kate's bedroom. He had a habit of owning any space he entered.

"Why torment yourself, my friend? Why not end her suffering?" The crimson rings around his dark irises suggested that although he had fed recently, the scent of blood oozing from Kate's open wounds affected him. It had been a thousand years since a vampire had given him the bite of immortality, and since then he had gained remarkable control over his bloodlust, but it was clearly strained by Katerina's weak, injured presence. She was easy prey. The only reason he hadn't sunk his fangs into her neck was as a favour to me.

And maybe because he knew that, as good a friend as he was, I would tear off his head before he reached her.

His gaze flicked towards me. "I would make it quick, and the pleasure she would feel in the interim has to be better than what she endures now."

"I know." My voice was rough, hoarse with anguish. "Perhaps it would be for the best, but I—" I gritted my teeth and bowed my head, leaning my elbows on my knees.

Adrian chuckled. "I never thought I'd see the day."

"It's not what you think."

"No? You interfered with the threads of fate. Gave up a part of yourself. How many times have you told me the price of doing so was too high to pay?"

A groan from the bed drew my gaze to Kate, and before I was aware of it, I was on my feet. I crossed the room and lowered myself onto the mattress, moving gently enough that I didn't disturb her.

"From the moment I saw her, my world shifted. I expected her to die, yet of all the people to survive that ritual, she was the one to walk away. To walk away with *me*, immune to my touch. Every single day since then, I've feared something would steal her from me. When she was lost in that fire, I felt the tether between us grow taut, and it ached more than anything I remember from my old life. I knew if it snapped, that ache would never fade. Not if centuries passed and I finally paid this debt. Whatever the consequences, I couldn't let her go."

Soul bared, exposed to the only other person on this earth I trusted, I looked up to meet Adrian's thoughtful gaze.

"In that case, we'll allow her to rest and recover," he said after a moment. "But some thought must be given to the future. You explained about the spell that bound her to you, but what does that mean for either of you? Fate clearly played a part in bringing you together, but what you choose to do with that gift remains in your hands. Do you mean to let the poor girl know how you feel?"

I huffed. "No, I don't think that would be in either of our best interests. Sixty years and she still grieves for what she's lost. I doubt the attentions of the spirit-herder who escorted her husband and son to the beyond would be appreciated."

Adrian frowned. "You do yourself too little credit."

I shook my head. "Leave it, will you? Allow me to steal what small pleasures I can from simply being in her company."

"And what exactly might that entail? Will you spend the rest of eternity watching over her? Saving her from whatever trouble she finds herself in? Death won't be pleased. Not only about you upsetting the balance or the stolen soul, but also its loyal servant falling off his duty. The terms of your deal will take more than you might be willing to give."

My gaze returned to Kate, to the shallow rise and fall of

her chest, the rapid pulse in her throat, the way her fingers twitched against the covers. I thought of what it would mean if another Shogaur came for her, or some other enemy that moved faster than the encroaching fire. Something that moved too quickly for me to step in and help her.

"I'm willing to give up enough to ensure she's protected. Once she's recovered, I mean to teach her how to save herself."

18

Katerina

Florence, Italy - August 1209

GRADUALLY, THE PAIN subsided and other sensations trickled in. The sweetness of cool water being poured into
my mouth; the spasm of lazy muscles as they worked to draw
the water down my throat; low, soft voices speaking over me.
One was unknown, and the other I now recognized as Emrick's.

Emrick? Was I dead? Was this stage of searing agony part
of crossing into the afterlife? If that was the case, had my
family suffered this badly when they'd died? Had their passing
been the same endless torture? I'd hoped they'd found peace
once their earthly torment was over, but now my heart bled
with the thought that they'd been trapped in this in-between

place where every pain was amplified.

"It seems your lovely lady is crying," the unfamiliar voice said.

The earth shifted beneath me, and a leathery hand rested over mine. "It's all right, Kate. You're safe, and you're healing," came Emrick's voice, a sweet balm against the tearing, raking assault of my grief. "Hurry back so we can start teaching you to be the sorceress you were meant to be."

My heart lurched at those words. At that voice saying those words. I wasn't dead, then. The news didn't fill me with excitement or a need to race back into wakefulness, but it did come as a relief that I wouldn't face endless years stuck in a world of torture.

I hung on to them as consciousness washed in and out, more discomfort fading, more movement returning to my body even if strength was still wanting.

Finally, the day came when I was able to open my eyes, and the first thing I saw was Emrick sitting in a chair beside my bed, his moonlight gaze resting on me with an expression so intense my heart fluttered, which in my weakened state made me cough, which in my healing state made me groan and curl onto my side as I held my middle together. Only then did I realize the straps around my wrists had been removed, and I wrapped my fingers around the bare skin. Bare, soft skin, pale and unblemished. As though I hadn't nearly burned to a final death.

"We had to strap you down," Emrick said, his voice as low and soft as it had been during the raging pain. The voice that had represented so many people I had loved and lost as it guided me back here. "As soon as your skin healed and you stopped flailing, we were able to release you."

"You saved me from the fire?" My voice was barely more than a rasp, as rough as crushed stone.

"I'm sorry I was so late." He bowed his head against the gloved hand wrapped around mine. "I should never have left you in the first place. I'm so sorry."

I stared at the top of his head, my pulse racing. I found myself longing to run my fingers through his golden blond hair, down his face, over his lips. Just to prove to myself he was really here. That he'd rescued me at the last when I'd believed all hope was gone.

"How long has it been?" I coughed again, and Emrick grabbed a cup from the table beside the bed. With one strong arm tucked behind my back, he helped me sit up enough to drink.

"A month. Maybe a little less."

A month unaware. A month of the Crusaders marching across Languedoc. How far had they spread? How many lives had been lost?

I looked around the room, not recognizing the solid, dark

furniture or the sounds of birdsong coming through the open balcony on the warm summer breeze. The scent of roses filled the air.

Roses for me, but what of Béziers?

"I couldn't stop Shogaur." Tears stung my eyes. "I used the words you taught me, but I couldn't banish him in time."

Emrick took the cup from my shaking hand, set it on the table, and wound his leather-bound fingers through mine. His thumb stroked my palm in a soothing, repetitive motion. "You did, Kate. The gates of hell swallowed him whole. He's gone."

I sucked in a breath as I raised my eyes to his and found only sincerity staring back at me. No lie to make me feel better. I'd won.

A smile threatened to cut through my grief until I remembered the Abbot and the marching soldiers. "What of the Crusade? What of the city? Jean and Edith?"

Now he dropped his gaze, and the grip on my hand tightened, no longer reassuring but bracing. "Shogaur's removal didn't stop them. They sacked the city. Slaughtered every last person within its walls."

Shock left me numb as I attempted to process what he was saying.

"That can't be. There were Catholics in that city. Their own. They couldn't have killed them all."

"Amalric had opinions on the subject," Emrick replied, his

tone dry, disgusted.

I didn't know what he meant by that, but I didn't care to know. All dead. Every last one of them. Just like what had happened in Palonia. Not even when I tried to save people could I make a difference.

"I don't think anything you did could have stopped them. Not once they started."

"It's still going on, isn't it?" I asked, not wanting to hear it but needing to know.

Emrick still refused to look at me. "It is. No magical influence, just humans giving in to their baser natures."

In other words, there was nothing I could do to help even if I had the strength to get out of this bed.

My stomach heaved, and I turned my head to bring up the water I'd just consumed. I swallowed the cries that wanted to burst from my chest, holding on to the pressure of them as earned torment. Tears streamed down my face as more water came out of my twisted, sickened guts. Emrick pulled my hair over my shoulder to keep it out of my face as I spat into the chamber pot.

Once I had nothing more to bring up, once the spasm in my chest eased and exhaustion claimed me, I drew back to him, my hands shaking—my whole body trembling. "Did you mean what you said before? About teaching me how to use my magic?"

"I did. I may not have magic of my own anymore—not the same kind, anyway—but maybe there's a way to work around that. I won't have you unable to protect yourself if I'm not there to help you." There seemed to be so much more he wanted to say, but all he added was, "I'll do my best to help you master your power. As for the rest, I know I taught you some basics with a blade, but I think it's time we broadened your knowledge. I have the perfect tutor lined up for you."

This tutor turned out to be a vampire, and on meeting him, it took all my will not to set him on fire and turn him to ash in the tradition of my people. He was, after all, our host in Florence, and it would have been a greater crime to return his hospitality with violence than it was for me to accept it. My parents would have to forgive me.

Adrian was a handsome man stuck in his mid-twenties, with brown hair that curled at the nape of his neck and dark eyes ringed in scarlet.

"Thank you for allowing me to stay while I recover," I said as he settled himself in the chair beside my bed.

"Emrick and I have known each other a long time." His accented words danced over his tongue like music. "Anyone important to him is a welcome guest in my home."

Despite his civility, I caught the hint of displeasure in the slight curl of his lip and the crease in his brow. Subtle, barely there in his flawless features, but clear enough to someone who felt like an interloper.

"You wish to learn the art of sword fighting?" he asked.

I bit my lip and raised my hand in front of me. "I wish to master my power." I summoned a low fireball that hovered over my palm, then crushed my fingers around it. My missing gloves were a hole in my heart, but I would learn to make do without them. "If Emrick believes weapons might serve me as well, then I'll gladly accept whatever training you wish to pass on."

He arched an eyebrow. "*Whatever* training?"

I narrowed my eyes. "I suppose that depends on what you have in mind." Host or not, there was only so far I was willing to go to let a vampire have his way.

A low chuckle rumbled in his throat. "Oh, I believe you and I will have great fun together, Katerina."

The way my name flicked over his tongue left goosebumps on my arms, and warmth filled my cheeks at his bright smile.

After that promise, whatever issue he had with my presence seemed to vanish. He visited my room every day, bringing books for me to read and a set of pipes that he played to entertain me until, finally, I was able to get out of bed.

He never revealed his true age, but by the way he spoke,

I guessed he was significantly older than he appeared. Old enough that he lacked the bloodlust that governed the younger of his kind. Hadn't I grown up listening to stories of the creatures of the night who emptied whole villages with their insatiable appetites? Hadn't my people trained from childhood to kill them on sight, along with every other type of creature that threatened to upset the balance between magical and mundane?

Over the months that passed, however, it became clear Adrian had risen above his instincts, or at least kept them so deeply buried I couldn't find fault with his behaviour. His human servants had nothing negative to say about him, his life within the stone walls of his estate remained free of the drama and violence that infested the city proper, and he was never anything but kind to me. He surrounded himself with books, art, music—everything he claimed appealed to the soul he'd lost at the time of his human death.

Every night, Adrian and I went into the massive gardens that stretched from the back of his towered estate and he pushed me to the brink of exhaustion, first with a sword before switching to daggers as a more likely weapon. Easy for a woman to hide on her person and only necessary as backup.

Because of course my magic would be my primary source of defence. If I could learn it, which I'd begun to doubt once again. After months of work, I hadn't progressed farther than the fireballs I'd learned to shoot from my hands despite

Emrick's frequent lessons.

To my surprise, the spirit-herder stayed true to his word, coming consistently every few days and rarely missing a day if he promised to be there. On those days, from the moment I woke up to the moment Adrian rose from his daytime sleep, Emrick stayed with me, correcting my form, suggesting ideas on how to open my mind and work past the doubts and fears he believed held me back.

Progress was painfully slow, but as the years passed, my strength grew, my knowledge deepened, and more than once I surprised us both with a successful show of control.

On days I didn't expect Emrick, I worked on my own, sitting in the sunshine when the weather was good, surrounded by flowers and the cheerful gurgle of a brook navigating its way through the earthy beds. I summoned fireballs that trailed up my arms before they left my skin to wind through the air around me. Three, four, five of them at a time, whirling around my head until I sucked the heat from them and turned them into ice balls I then projected into the stone wall that encircled the garden.

Without my gloves, my control was precarious, each simple manoeuvre taking twice the concentration. Over time, I learned to work without them, but their absence remained a sore point.

By the end of my fifth year, the garden wall was scored by thousands of ice strikes, and I watched them multiply with pride even as Adrian shook his head at the damage to his home. He said nothing, though, and by the gleam in his eye and the faint upwards twist of his mouth, I suspected he was as proud of my achievements as I was.

It turned out not everything my family had taught me about vampires was true. He was far more than a mindless monster. He loved to laugh, loved to learn, loved to dance.

While we began our acquaintance blade to blade, we began our friendship hand to hand in the vast hall of his estate with the extra training he'd alluded to during our first meeting: dance lessons.

He filled my wardrobe with gowns the likes of which I'd never seen, let alone worn, and though his personal staff was small—no other vampires, only a handful of servants who kept the place tidy during the day and thralls to serve his needs at night—for the first time in my life, I had a personal maid who made me feel like a queen.

For those first few years, life was more idyllic than it had any right to be. The burden I carried with me never lessened. In fact, it grew weightier after the events in Languedoc and as I devoured news of the Crusade that continued to ruin so many lives. My guilt, my failure, hung on my shoulders like a mantle not even the softest wool or brightest silks could replace. Especially not here, living in this large, mostly empty estate with more luxuries than I'd ever dreamed existed.

To escape my deep sense of hopelessness, I focused on my studies, devouring everything there was to know about the era in which I now lived, sixty years after I should have died with my family. I was over ninety years old, yet I hadn't aged a day past twenty-four.

Adrian taught me the language and history of the region, the customs of the nobility and those of the peasantry. I learned how to fit in no matter where I went, blending in to avoid questions or suspicions about who or what I was.

Emrick helped where he could, though he left most of the work to Adrian, who'd made a point to tell me that after centuries of knowing Emrick, this was the first time he'd seen his friend spend any extended time in this world. He smiled when he said it, a knowing glint in his brown-and-crimson eyes, but he never brought me into his secret.

Whatever it was that amused Adrian, I was grateful for Emrick's presence. Even more so than before the events in France, he had become a source of light in the darkness. Not once but twice guiding me to safety and always there to watch over me. A few hours a day a few times a week was all he spent with me, never touching me, saying little, but I looked forward to those few hours from the time I woke up. He usually left with the sunset, leaving me to Adrian's company, and I suspected the reason he left so early was to avoid his friend's urgings for him to join us in a dance.

My favourite nights were when he stayed. Adrian would grab his lute and strum some new melody he'd picked up, and Emrick would pull out his pipes, and between the two of them, the evening would be filled with the sweetest music that made me wish time would stand still.

Which it had for us, in a way, the three of us living outside the world inhabited by those blessed with mortality, standing as though frozen while life twisted and whirled around us with the span of years.

Almost seven years had passed before, one night, Adrian hooked his arm through mine as we stood on the balcony and said, "When you arrived here, I didn't think I would find such pleasure in a living, breathing housemate, but you've revived my love of this world, Katerina."

I chuckled and squeezed his arm. "It's nice to see I've achieved something, then."

"Ah, I see great things in store for you, cuore mio. As for me, now that I know you're safe and comfortable, I believe it's time for life to resume."

He didn't explain what he meant, but after that night, Adrian began leaving his estate, often for days at a time. He never told me where he was going, but he would come home covered in blood and oozing satisfaction.

Emrick would often disappear for longer stretches while Adrian was gone, leaving me curious and frustrated at their secrets.

"Where do you run off to?" I finally asked Adrian as he led me through the steps of a new dance.

"Ah, mia Katerina," he said, bending to press a kiss on the back of my hand. "You do not want to trouble yourself with my comings and goings. You're happy here, are you not?"

"I am. You know I am. But that doesn't mean I don't indulge in curiosity while you're away."

He chuckled and carried us through a few more steps. "Where do you think I go?"

I wrinkled my nose. "To feed? To plague some village far from here so it can't be traced back to you as you go door to door and drink every young virgin dry?"

He threw back his head with a laugh and draped an arm around my shoulders, leading me outside into the garden. "What an imagination you have. A few hundred years ago, you might have been correct, but my tastes run less towards virgins these days and more towards villains."

"What sort of villains? Are you an avenging angel, feeding off those who cause harm to others?"

I asked the question with dramatic flair, fully expecting him to laugh again and discount my fancies, but to my surprise, his smile faded into seriousness, and he turned away from me to stare up at the moon.

"Do you have any regrets, Kate?"

"Thousands."

He nodded. "Then you understand in a way our friend does not. Emrick has been outside this world for so long, he no longer appreciates what it means to be a part of it. I, on the other hand, watch it all with deep remorse. There's so much beauty in life, and I have done my fair share in destroying it. First as a soldier, then as a fledgling vampire. Rivers of blood trail in my shadow, and nothing I do will ever make up for it." He shifted to face me, and I caught the red swimming in his eyes. He hadn't fed lately. "Yet I *try*, Katerina. That is what I do while I'm gone. The villains I seek are not the humans who harm their neighbours for greed or lust, but the magical creatures that prey on the unsuspecting. Threats as I once was."

The irony almost made me laugh, that this vampire, evil in the eyes of my community, should dedicate himself to the same mission of protection and balance as Palonia once had.

I thought of Shogaur, his hunger for fear and the damage he'd caused in his pursuit of a filling meal. If Adrian had been in France at the time, he might have stopped him earlier than I had. Maybe before the demon had reached the Pope's ear. Before anyone had to die for his survival.

I could have done it if I'd known what I did now.

Perhaps with Adrian's help, I could finally succeed in making up for the failures of my past.

"The next time you leave, I want to go, too," I said.

His expression flickered, jumping through surprise to horror before landing on intrigued acceptance. "Very well. Though you'll have to convince Emrick it's a good idea, because I suspect if I suggest it, I'll be staring at my final death."

19

Katerina

ADRIAN WAS RIGHT, of course. The moment I mentioned my intentions to Emrick, he crossed his arms and widened his stance, and his eyes shuttered.

"I don't think so."

I mirrored his pose. "Excuse me? I don't believe I was asking you for permission."

"Of course not. Why ask permission to get eaten by some wyvern or burned alive by another demon?"

"Adrian wouldn't let that happen. Besides, isn't this why you agreed to help me develop my magic? So I could defend myself?"

"Defend yourself, yes. From enemies coming after you. Not so you can run into the unknown looking for trouble. If I'd known that was where your interests lay, I would have left you in ignorance to spend your days here among the flowers."

His voice was a growl, his silver eyes flashing, like clouds passing over the moon, and in the face of his surliness, his immediate dismissal of my request, my anger flared.

"If that's true, you should have let me burn." I kept my voice low, fighting to keep it level. "What sort of eternity awaits me if all I can do is sit around? Why did you come back? Why did you save me if all you wanted to do was tuck me away somewhere and leave me again?"

It had been seven years since that day, and I'd never found the courage to ask him. I likely wouldn't have if my frustration hadn't pushed the words out of me. Though the second they hung between us, my breath caught in my throat. I found myself torn between dread and hope that he might actually answer.

Heart thudding against my ribs, blood rushing under the surface of my skin, I waited as he stared at me, his lips parted as though on the verge of speaking but uncertain what to say. His whole body seemed to tense, and for the barest moment, his gaze dropped to my lips.

Then he squeezed his eyes shut with a scowl, I released my breath, and time resumed as though it had never taken that oh-so-brief hiatus.

Emrick might pretend it hadn't happened, but I couldn't ignore it. My head reeled with thoughts and desires I'd believed long behind me. Six decades I'd walked beside this man, but only now was I waking up to the connection that existed alongside our bond—and the vague hope that it might lead to something more.

Guilt chased the desire, a sense of betraying my family by wishing for happiness when they'd suffered because of my lack of action, but the war within me waged without my permission.

Not that I would get my wish. That was clear by the way Emrick stepped away from me and shoved his hand through his loose hair. It swept just shy of his broad shoulders, the sunlight catching the soft red woven through the rich gold. "You're an infuriating woman. Fine. You want to run back into the fire and see if something else can get as close to killing you as Shogaur did? Let's begin. From here, we double your lessons. I won't have you facing cockatrices and vampires and sorcerers with only some daggers and a few fireballs."

It wasn't an answer to my question, but as he was offering part of what I wanted, I didn't push it. Though my curiosity burned more than ever as to what else he might have wanted to say.

Or what I wanted him to say.

We set out for the gardens where we did our usual training,

but there was no relaxed pace today. Instead of gentle guidance and soft encouragement, I got demands and impatience. I was reminded of my teachers in Palonia after they realized I'd never amount to anything, and though it killed whatever confidence the last seven years had instilled in me, I found myself pushing against him, rising to meet his demands, ignoring the impatience.

"More fire. Come on, Kate, you're fighting demons here. They'll kill you if you don't hit them first. They've got you surrounded. You think three little fireballs will destroy them?"

I breathed deeply into my magic to drag more of it out of me, determined to show him I wasn't helpless.

But the more magic I channelled, the more drained I felt, with only a few extra fireballs to show for it.

"I need to stop for today. I'm pulling at dregs."

"Stop running away from your power like a scared little child," he said.

"I'm not." Rage bubbled in my chest, a frustrating distraction as my next wave of fire fizzled into nothing before it left my hand.

"I'm watching it happen. I feel it in the air. The hum of power that vibrates against my bones until my teeth shake—then it disappears moments before you let go. Stop hiding in excuses and in the belief that you can't do it."

I gritted my teeth and tried to tune him out. He had no idea what he was talking about. I'd always been aware of my power. I wasn't afraid of it.

"Your whole life you've put pressure on yourself to live up to everyone else's expectations, and it's stifled you. Stop working for anyone else. Stop trying to be who anyone else wants you to be. Your power is your own. Only you know what you can do with it."

More magic, more fire. I was exhausted, and although my attack was strong enough to reach the leaves on the trees, it was a pathetic demonstration. I was too tired and too angry, my concentration too buried beneath the urge to throw a giant fireball directly into his gorgeous face.

"You come from a line of incredible sorcerers, Kate, how could the same power not run in your veins? *Own it.* You're the only one holding yourself back. Own. It."

Sweat streamed down my temples as I pulled more fire into my hands, and with a cry of release, I sent it forth. It spilled from my palms and swept around me and out, and a shriek pierced the garden as one of the servants rushed away from the blast that carried through the air and extinguished against the stone wall.

I stumbled forward, out of breath, shocked at what I'd done, worried I'd hurt the woman only to watch in relief as she rushed to the side door to escape inside, throwing us a backwards glance as she went.

My heart thudded in my chest and my blood simmered with exultation as I turned to Emrick. He stood on the edge of the garden, untouched by the fire, arms crossed, face blank. For a heartbeat, we stared at each other until a spark danced in his eyes and a small smile graced his perfect lips.

"Now that, sorceress, is what I'm talking about."

From that moment, my training began in earnest, and I realized how soft he'd been with me for the past seven years. Those lessons had been novice level, the sort of thing I should have learned as a child. Now that I'd fully embraced my power after decades of thinking I already had, we stepped into the intermediate lessons.

After three days of endless hounding, pushing myself until I dropped into bed exhausted, too tired for dancing or weapons training, I was ready to give up. Emrick could get what he wanted, and I would live in the garden forever.

Become one with the flowers, pretty and nice-smelling and never having to move again.

"Get up," Emrick said, appearing out of the mist next to my bed.

Based on the way the sun fell into my room through the open balcony, it wasn't even noon, which was far too early based on the schedule I kept in a vampire's home.

I grunted, rolled over to put my back to him, and pulled up the covers. "You win. I quit. I'm too sore to learn anything else."

"No, no, Kat, you don't get to quit now. Not after I've invested this much effort into you."

"I still prefer Kate, actually."

"Kat suits you better. Especially when your claws come out."

I flashed him a rude hand gesture over my shoulder, then pulled my pillow over my head.

The pillow disappeared with a jerk, and I gasped as I sat up to see what he'd done with it. The covers fell and pooled around my waist. "Pardon me very much."

Modesty was not a virtue we'd bothered with in Palonia, but my skin grew hot when I caught the flash of hunger in Emrick's eyes at the sight of my naked skin. Unless I imagined it, because a moment later it was gone, his silver eyes void of emotion.

"I got something for you." The mist opened beside him as he reached into some unseen afterlife nook.

Curious, I shifted on the bed to face him, doing him the favour of pulling the sheets up to cover my chest.

But all thought of his comfort disappeared when he pulled a wooden box roughly half an arm span in length and two hands in width into this world. The dark, polished mahogany gleamed in the sunlight, and even from here, the magic wafted off it in waves that danced between the hairs on my arms.

"What is it?"

I couldn't help myself. I felt like a child on a festival day, awaiting gifts from the elders.

He held the box out to me, and I snatched it from him, resting it on my crossed legs so I could use both hands to open it.

Inside, on a bed of soft green velvet, lay my gloves.

The runes that helped me channel my magic shone with their faintly silver hue. The leather had been recently oiled. They blurred in my vision as tears welled in my eyes.

"How is this possible? The soldiers took them. They've been gone for years."

Emrick shrugged and crossed his arms. "It occurred to me the other day they might still be at the church where Shogaur held you. You told me they couldn't be destroyed by time or fire, so the chances were pretty good. I went to take a look and found them stuffed in a drawer."

The only possession I'd kept of my old life had been stolen from me, and now, by some miracle, they'd been restored.

No, not *some* miracle. This man.

This incredible man who'd thought of me and gone out of his way to look for them. How had he known how much I missed them? I hadn't said anything, had accepted their loss even as I mourned them. Yet somehow he knew.

"Thank you." It came out as barely more than a whisper, but by the slight shift of his shoulders, he'd heard me.

It wasn't enough, though. No quiet words were sufficient to express how grateful I was. Without thinking, I set the box aside and threw myself out of bed to latch my arms around his waist. My nose brushed against his white shirt, and I inhaled the rich scents of campfire and loam that made my mouth water. Delicious, familiar. Home.

He held his arms extended by his sides, his wide frame frozen against mine, until he relaxed and slid his hands across my back, clasping me to him.

I pulled back without letting him go, and my gaze trailed along the curve of his collarbones where they appeared from under his shirt, up the smooth lines of his neck, his jaw, his lips, and lingered there.

After a few breaths of our hearts beating side by side, he cleared his throat. "I thought we'd move on to lightning today."

It wasn't what I'd expected him to say, but a shiver ran through me at his words, nonetheless. Lightning? That was impossible.

Almost as impossible as the feelings for Emrick I was struggling to admit to myself.

"I don't have that kind of power," I said. "Believe me, if I did, my father would have known. Lightning was his specialty."

Emrick laughed gruffly as he pulled away, his gaze firmly on mine. The air cleared between us, and I didn't know if I was more relieved at the moment passing or disappointed it had ended.

"I don't know if it was your parents who brought you up badly, your teachers who failed you, or you who failed yourself, but you seem to live under a few vast misconceptions. If you care to undo any of them, come find me in the garden. Otherwise, feel free to go back to sleep."

He left, closing the door behind him. After the shortest of hesitations, I drew on my gloves and set about getting dressed.

A large part of me didn't believe him, but a larger part was beginning to accept that so much of what I'd believed was wrong—and it was time to find out if he was right.

20

Katerina

Florence, Italy - September 1216

I DIDN'T BOTHER with layers of skirts or fabrics, settling for a simple shift belted at the waist—a nicer, washed version of the garment Shogaur's minions had stuffed me into but comfortable in the stifling summer heat and more flexible for moving about.

As he'd promised, Emrick was in our usual spot. He stood staring into the brook, his arms crossed, a deep furrow between his brows. I stopped and watched him for a heartbeat—two, three—wondering what he was thinking about that made him look so serious and admiring his defined physique beneath the rough-worked shirt and leather breeches. His hair was pulled back at his neck, tied with a leather strap, but a few strands had fallen free and blew about in the soft, sweet-scented breeze. He wore his gloves, of course. I so rarely saw him without them that they seemed as much a part of him as mine were.

Again, that sense of familiarity swept over me. Of finally finding the roots I had wanted to set down in France. A safe place in the chaos.

That had to be why I was so drawn to him, so lost in his silver eyes I often felt as though I were caught in the tide, unable to escape him even if I wanted to.

Or was that the bond?

Was anything I felt for him real, or was it the twisted magic that linked my life to his?

Whatever the reason, I didn't know what to make of these urges awakening within me after lying dormant for so many decades. Whenever he stepped through the mist, carrying the sun with him despite the grungy murk of the afterlife, my stomach fluttered and I felt alive in ways I hadn't in so long.

He'd always made it clear that contact was unwanted, so regardless of the yearning in my heart, I would ensure our relationship remained as it was. Bonded and bound. Teacher and student. Occasional transport.

Ignoring the ache of disappointment as I reached my decision, I crossed the garden towards him.

"All right, *gàst-ladman*. You say I can harness lightning? Let's see you prove it."

He turned to face me, and whatever dark thoughts haunted him disappeared from his features under another flash of hunger that stole my breath and mocked my choice to remain indifferent. He blinked and the desire was gone, replaced by a cocky amusement as he gestured for me to take my spot.

I stood in the empty patch of garden, long cleared of any nearby flowers for me to incinerate, and drew in three deep breaths. With every exhale, I allowed my body to relax. It had become a sort of ritual at the beginning of these sessions, one Emrick had tried on multiple occasions to rid me of—"You won't have time to breathe if the enemy is charging at you. You need to be ready to strike on a whim"—but one I'd kept despite him.

Or maybe to spite him.

The air shifted as he circled the clearing to come up behind me. Although he made no physical contact, I was hyper-aware of him standing so close the heat of his chest brushed against my shoulder blades through my shift. His breath fanned the back of my neck, sending a rush of sparks under my skin down into my core.

I longed for him to close the gap between us, to run his lips over my shoulder and curl his hands into my hips as he pressed himself against me.

The intensity of my desire in response to that longing

knocked me out of my deep breathing with a gasp, and my eyes flew open to see a hint of his profile as he peered over my left shoulder.

A moment later, his gloved hand tapped my right arm. "Even in a quiet garden, the breathing doesn't help you. You're too tense. Relax or you won't achieve anything, and you'll tell me I was wrong when the fault is entirely yours."

The lustful ache faded under his teasing, and I stuck my tongue out at the air where I knew he wouldn't see it. In years lived, I was inching close to one hundred, but this man brought out my immaturity like no one had in decades.

"Now, I won't lie. Lightning is challenging, especially if you're used to focusing inward, as most fire users are. Until now, we've used your blood as a focal point, the heat in your veins that channels your magic and drives the flame to your hands. All imagery, of course. The only power inside you is your magic. The fire doesn't exist until you bring it forth."

I gritted my teeth, wishing I could block out this part of his lecture. The last thing I needed was for his training to confuse everything I'd learned about my primary element.

"Lightning is all about what's in the air. It's a recognition and manipulation of your surroundings. We'll start with something familiar. Close your eyes."

I did as he said, and as the garden disappeared from view, his delicious smell grew stronger. I breathed it in, enjoying the way it swirled in my chest and slid lower into my stomach. The longing to follow the smell to its source, to bury my nose in Emrick's neck and wrap myself in the comfort it provided, nearly overwhelmed me, but I forced my attention back to what he was saying.

"Focus on the wind." His lips were close to my ear, his breath stirring my hair. "The constant movement, the way it brushes along your skin. Notice the moisture hiding unseen within it. This same moisture you manipulate when you reverse your heat to freeze your surroundings. Do you think you form ice from nothing? It's the water in the air that you're turning to your will. Try it."

Under the steady cadence of his voice, any doubt in my ability became nothing more than a shadow behind me. All I saw was possibility. If he told me to create a unicorn out of the flowers, I would do it without trouble.

I raised my hand and absorbed the heat from the air, aware of the pull in the atmosphere as the droplets drew from seemingly nothing to form ice crystals on my palm.

I projected enough heat for them to melt, then reformed them, taking note of the differences in the air as to what froze and what didn't, and after hours of meditating on the shifting sensations of freezing and melting, I realized Emrick was right—there was water everywhere.

"Now that you sense it, I want you to use it." Emrick's

voice remained low, remained close, and the sound travelled straight down between my legs, causing my knees to tremble. "Reach past yourself, past what you believe your limitations to be. Whatever you want to freeze, do it."

My history and experience pushed me to question him, but he hadn't been wrong so far, so I held out my hand and focused on the air above it. Close enough that I hoped to trick my mind into following through the way it always did while challenging myself to push harder and break into something new.

For the longest time, nothing happened. I reached out to sense the changes in the atmosphere I'd noticed before, and although I was aware of them, I couldn't connect from a distance to manipulate them.

The sun had passed its peak by the time I felt a surge of magic and noticed a slight shimmer in the emptiness in front of me. My breath caught in my throat, and I looked at Emrick over my shoulder. His eyes met mine, as though he'd been watching me the entire time.

"Did you see that?" I was unable to hold back my giddiness. "I saw it change."

He smiled, amusement dancing across his features. "Then I'd say you should keep working at it. There's nothing preventing you from reaching greatness, and we have all the time in the world."

With his confidence at my back and excitement at my progress in my heart, I returned my attention to my outstretched hand and the air above it and reached out again. This time, it was a simple matter to sense the water and twist it to my will, cooling it, hardening it, until snowflakes danced around me despite the early autumn heat.

I laughed and stretched out my arms as I spun in a circle through the snow, expending more magic to create more flakes. Soon, the grass at our feet was covered in a spattering of winter.

"Incredible!" I said when I came to a stop facing Emrick. "I've never done anything like this before, not once in my whole life. My mother—" At the thought of my family, my heart clenched with its old, familiar scars. My smile faltered, but I did my best to hold it steady. "She would have been very impressed. Ice was her focus."

"That explains why you're so creative with it."

I frowned, confused, and he gestured to the grass. When I looked down, I realized the snow had fallen in decorative swirls that no one would believe were natural.

"I didn't mean to do that. But that's what she used to do. Sometimes she'd freeze the lake in patterns and send the children running across it to gather the flowers of ice she left for us." I chuckled. "It was a good way to keep us out of trouble while the adults went hunting."

Memories flowed around me with the remaining snowflakes, though by the time the last trace of snow melted, I'd buried them and reformed the walls around my heart.

"But we didn't come here to learn ice," I reminded Emrick. "You promised lightning."

He dipped his chin. "I did indeed. We begin as we always do."

I turned around to face the wall and resumed my meditative stance—feet apart, hands at my sides, eyes closed.

Emrick's warmth brushed against my back, and I sank as much into his heat as his presence. "Just as you found the water in the air, the lightning is always there as well. Think of the sparks that fly from your fingers when you pick up a woolen cloak. Think of the energy in the air when a storm rages. Just like with fire and with water, the elements are at your fingertips. It's not a matter of *whether* you can access them but *how* you access them. So again, focus on the air, but instead of noticing the wind, notice the stillness beneath the wind. The way the world becomes so calm and quiet, like the moment before thunder rolls across the sky. The tingle on your skin, the pull on your hair."

Once again, his voice lulled me into a state of deep relaxation until he was all I heard, my awareness filled by the vibration of his voice. I struggled to move beyond it to do as he said, and it took until he fell silent to wrap my thoughts around the sensations he'd described.

The sun was full west now, shining right in my face,

warming my cheeks, drying the remaining snowflakes. And with the melt, I detected something else I hadn't noticed before. The faint sense of dryness tugging the moisture out of my skin beyond the disappearing snow. It brought up thoughts of chapped hands and scaly flesh in the dead of winter, the pain in my lungs when I took a deep breath on a cold day.

I latched on to the feeling but didn't rush, not wanting to disappoint myself by attempting anything before I was ready.

"The difference with lightning," Emrick said after a long bout of easy silence, "is it needs something to connect with. Unlike ice or fire that can sit in your hand, lightning cannot be held. It's an arc that jumps from source to target, there and gone." He reached his arm around me and wrapped his fingers around my right hand. My pulse leapt at the contact. Carefully, he positioned my fingers so they curved towards each other, as though I were holding a ball. The leather of his gloves was rough against my bare fingertips, and goosebumps spread up my arms and over the back of my neck. "It's easiest to begin with sparks. All it requires is a close distance and enough focus to release your magic in a wave that bounces between your fingers. With enough time and practice, you can spit those sparks outwards the same way you do your fire."

At his description, I thought of my father standing on the bank of the lake, facing down a cockatrice that had come too close to the village. Ice hadn't slowed the creature down and fire couldn't reach it, but my father refused to give up. He'd stood still and confident as the cockatrice charged, and before it reached him, he released three bolts of lightning. Two struck the beast straight on, forcing it back, and the third caught the water behind it. Blue-purple-white, the lightning had danced across the surface on its own.

The fallout had been devastating, but no one could deny it had been effective.

I wasn't striving for devastating. Not yet. All I wanted was proof that with time and practice, I could take down a charging cockatrice without flinching and be as brave and self-assured as my father had been.

So I focused on the air, ignored the moisture, and sought out the stillness. My heartbeat slowed, and my breaths grew deep and even, as though everything around me were as quiet as the energy I chased.

Emrick never moved. He stood so close that every once in a while his chest brushed my shoulder blades as his breath caressed my neck. His nearness interrupted my concentration, threw off my measured breathing, made my heartbeat hitch, but I didn't want him to back up, even if it meant we had to stand here all night while I wrangled my power to do what I wanted. I worried that if he stepped away, I would lose whatever confidence I'd gained over the course of the day.

When something brushed the back of my head—was he

smelling my hair?—my pulse leapt, and a sharp pain zapped my fingers. I jumped with a tiny shriek and bumped into Emrick's chest. He grasped my shoulders to steady me, his grip tight, his fingers curling into my flesh just as I'd wanted them to do around my hips. I expected him to let go as soon as he realized what he'd done, knowing how much he didn't enjoy touching me, but my breath stuttered when he stayed still.

All thought vanished under the weight of his hands, the heat of his gloved palms searing my skin through the thin sleeves of my shift. I swallowed hard and tried to remember what I was doing, but my entire body trembled.

"Breathe, Katerina," he said into my ear, a humourous lilt in his voice. "It's the foundation of any good magic."

I chuckled dryly. "I see, so I can only breathe on your terms, is that it? When I try to breathe on mine, it's a crutch that will get me killed."

"There are a lot of things I prefer done on my terms, Kat. You surviving is not one of them."

My heart thrashed against my ribs, and I squeezed my eyes shut as the ground swayed beneath me. But as I'd done all day, I obeyed my teacher's instructions and drew in a breath, releasing it gradually in an effort to slow my racing heart and refocus my energy.

"Kate," I reminded him absently, and his laugh rumbled in my ear.

He finally released me, and disappointment pooled in my stomach as the heat of his palms dissipated into the air.

Once more detached, alone, I settled into my body, following the pulses and surges of magic where they fluttered around my heart and mixed with my excitement and that deeper flurry of yearning. For a while, I enjoyed the sensation, allowing it to play, tickling my mind in ways I hadn't felt in far too long.

As the magic burrowed deeper, filling my marrow and stretching to the tips of my fingers and toes, I turned my thoughts to the world around me.

In my distraction, I'd lost track of the stillness. The water danced in the air, brushing against the hair on my arms, but the layers beyond escaped me, and the harder I tried to reach for them, the farther they scurried away.

It was only when Emrick's hand brushed my hip and my breath caught that I stopped trying so hard and latched on to the quiet.

A spark jumped between my thumb and middle finger. There was no denying it. My eyes had seen it. My fingers had most certainly felt it.

I'd worked lightning.

With a whoop of joy, I spun around to face Emrick, a wide smile stretching my cheeks. "You were right. I never believed it was possible, but I did it. Thank you. I couldn't have done it without you."

When I caught the darkening of his eyes, I realized how close we were standing, front to front, the top of my head only just reaching his shoulder so I had to tilt my head back to meet his silver stare. His gaze dropped to my lips. His chest was steel, as though he were holding his breath. As I watched, the black centres of his eyes spread until only a ring of moonlight remained around the edges. Any further words dried on my tongue, my heart beating too quickly to form my next thought.

"Anything is possible for you, Katerina. A few sparks is only the beginning. Once you believe it, once you embrace it, you'll make the world tremble. No one will dare stand in your way."

Sparks of a different variety lit up like fireflies in my blood, swirling and zapping in a downward spiral from my heart to my core, and my toes curled. I couldn't breathe. My skin sang, begging to be touched, begging for the impossible to become possible, just as Emrick promised.

The setting sun spilled its light across the garden in waves of red and gold, and the flower-scented breeze tousled my hair and danced through my shift. Every detail imprinted itself on my mind, marking this moment for the change it was.

I didn't know what to do. My body begged me to act on this wild desire, but my mind fought against seeking pleasure when I didn't deserve happiness. My heart rebelled against forcing my attentions on someone who had made it clear time and again that he had no interest in being anything other than a guardian, a mentor. I could want him, but I'd be more likely to get Adrian to respond to me that way than Emrick.

Despite all that, I couldn't pull away, held in place by an unseen force that channelled life into my blood the closer I stood to him.

He bent his head, and I parted my lips, longing to give in to the need for contact. For connection.

But before I got either, he closed his eyes, bowed his head on a sigh, and stepped back.

"I think that's enough for one day," he said. "We'll start again tomorrow."

The temperature dropped as the mist opened behind him, and he stepped through, leaving me alone in the sunset.

21

Katerina

Florence, Italy - October 1216

EMRICK DIDN'T COME back the next day. Or the day after that.

It was weeks before I saw him again, and every day, I wondered if it was his responsibilities or what had nearly happened in the garden that kept him away. But as much as doubt and regret and embarrassment ate at me, I didn't let his absence get in the way of my training. Every morning from the time I got up to the time Adrian rose, I practiced with fire, ice, and lightning. Working with Emrick's hints, I also tried to extend myself to manipulating water and air, and although I made some progress on the latter—mostly by manipulating the moisture and stillness I'd already learned—water remained out of my reach. Not that I was too surprised by this. No one in my community had been blessed with that particular skill, so it stood to reason I wouldn't be, either. I had a certain amount of control as it was freezing, but that was my limit.

For now.

Unless Emrick knew something I didn't and returned one day to tell me.

Adrian seemed amused by the spirit-herder's absence, something I chalked up to his strange, out-dated sense of humour. Fortunately for me, he didn't intend to let Emrick's disappearance interrupt our plans.

Within the first week of Emrick leaving and me practicing my sparks, Adrian invited me to join him in the hunt for a basilisk up north. It had lured more than one merchant caravan into its lair and terrorized the nearby village for months after making its home in the Alps. I jumped at the opportunity, excited to experience a hunt for myself.

Most Palonian sorcerers went on their first missions by the time they were twelve years old, learning from the elders. The best hunters saw over a hundred hunts between the time they were children to the time they finally retired and turned their purpose to guarding the village from external threats.

Because of my inability to develop my power, I'd never been invited to join them. I would have been a liability, more likely to cause someone harm than to help them.

Although I still couldn't claim mastery of my skills, Adrian never expressed doubt in my being a useful addition to his mission, and I was more grateful to him for that simple, silent confidence than I would ever be able to express.

For my first time out, my role would be simple: keep the basilisk distracted to give Adrian an opening to attack.

"Its underbelly is its weak spot," he said. "Gain the high ground if you can and keep its attention on you. Hopefully it won't see me coming until it's too late."

We found the giant snake tucked in a wooded valley near the mountains not long after sunset.

Under the glow of the moon, it lay still in the grass, stretching the length of nine tall men lying head to toe, and as thick around as four men lying on top of each other. Its fangs were the length of my arm, dripping venom every time its forked tongue shot out to taste the air, and its eyes… well, I was smart enough to know not to look into them.

It was possible my turn to stone wouldn't be permanent, but it was also possible I would be frozen in place, alive and aware. The thought of spending eternity as a living statue was enough to keep my gaze focused on the ground.

I didn't need to see the creature to feel the breadth of its power bearing down on me. The magic was like a heavy woollen cloak soaking up the air in the valley, leaving my breath shallow and quick.

Or perhaps that was the rush of battle.

Or the terror.

When I'd asked to accompany Adrian, I'd sworn I was ready, that my fight with Shogaur had taught me a few things. Now that I was here, faced with the possibility of being eaten and digested in a snake's innards, or impaled through the heart by a venomous fang, or getting my ribs crushed into pulp by the snake's enormous tail, I wasn't so sure.

Adrian left my side in a blur of speed that made it impossible for me to follow his movements. I wiped my palms on my thighs to dry them before summoning my magic, reaching first for the moisture in the air, freezing it into knives of ice that I hurled towards the basilisk's face. If we could damage its eyes, we would take out its greatest weapon.

In the darkness, I struggled to aim, and the ice blades struck off the creature's face without leaving a mark. I had no time to throw more before it whipped its tail at me and caught me across the gut, hurling me into the side of the mountain. My head slammed against the rock, sending lights bursting through my vision, and I slumped to the ground. The basilisk darted its head towards an attacking Adrian, but the vampire was too quick for it. Blackened blood sprayed as either blade or nails scored the basilisk's scales, and then Adrian was out of reach.

I shook myself off and summoned more ice into my

hands, holding the frozen shards this time to give myself more control. I needed to get closer, higher, but how to do that without getting right in the creature's face escaped me. Was there a way to pin it down?

As my pulse raced and the blood rushed in my ears, my vision focused on the smallest details in the darkness. I scanned the valley and took in the shadowed shapes of low-hanging branches, the fallen tree trunks, the few boulders lying scattered where they'd rolled down the mountain. Adrian had the strength to use them as weapons, but short of setting the branches on fire, I'd have to work around them.

The ice shards melted in my hands, pushing me to think faster. What would my parents have done?

Well, for one thing, they would have had a team of sorcerers working with them, so perhaps it wasn't fair of me to ask, but even so, they'd been resourceful, and I was their daughter.

My eye fell on one of the fallen trees, then back to the basilisk as it slithered in the direction Adrian had last been seen. It had clearly dismissed me as a threat—fair considering my poor first impression—but I was determined to make it regret its oversight.

Trying not to think too much about what I was doing or all the ways it might go wrong, I ran across the uneven ground to the fallen tree, leapt onto it at its base, and scurried up the length of the trunk, gaining height as well as distance. When I reached the end, as far as it would hold me, I waited until the basilisk came close enough, jumped onto its back, and drove the ice shards through its scales to anchor myself.

By sheer bad luck and misjudged aim, I'd fallen far enough down that I was barely able to roll out of the way as it turned its head to snap at me. My hand slipped off one of the ice shards, and I tightened my grip on the other to ensure I didn't fly off the creature as it undulated beneath me in its rush to reach Adrian, who flew at its face again.

Once this fight was over, I would take a moment to bask in the wonder of my friend's skills. For now, I kept my attention on helping him survive.

I grabbed the opportunity of its distraction to swing onto its back, pulled one shard free and drove the other in farther up. One by one, right then left, I used the shards to climb its scales, eventually reaching high enough that it couldn't whip around to snap at me, though that didn't stop it from trying. More than once, I nearly took another flight into the mountainside, and only by freezing my hands to the ice shards did I manage to hang on.

The metallic taste of blood burned the back of my throat, strong enough that I didn't know if it was my racing heart or if I'd bitten my tongue in my leap onto the basilisk's back. My muscles flexed, my stomach felt light, and my hands trembled with a mixed sense of invincibility and a certainty that I was going to die. But I was in it now, too far to back out.

Adrian must have registered what I was attempting because he never let up his assault, coming in from all sides and speeding away just as quickly. Every once in a while, a fresh cut swelled on the basilisk's front as the vampire got a strike in, but the snake never slowed down.

I reached its head, and my balance on the creature grew more precarious. I stayed in a low crouch to try to keep my footing and crept to its brow. It thrashed its head to sweep me off, and my foot slipped. I slammed the shard into its skull to hold myself in place, but now I was left dangling from the head of a snake, my feet unable to find purchase anywhere except close to its mouth, something I didn't want to test.

The basilisk shook its head again, and I squeezed my eyes shut as one of its great orbs came dangerously close.

What a sight I must have made hanging here, struggling to pull myself up. If Emrick were here, would he have laughed at my plight? I suspected so. If I survived this, Adrian would undoubtedly mention it later with that not-quite-there smirk of his.

But what did it matter what either of them thought? I wasn't counting myself out of the battle yet.

Using my upper body strength—which had improved thanks to Adrian's training but was still nothing to brag about—I heaved myself onto the basilisk's head. Out of breath, arms shaking, legs wobbly, I ran up the skull and stabbed a shard into its left eye.

It hissed and thrashed, its fangs snapping as it tried to reach me. I curled my fingers around the massive, tightly layered scales, winced as they sliced into my fingers, and held on as though my life depended on staying in place. Which it very well might have if I fell too close to those teeth.

Adrian made another assault, the basilisk snapped forward, and again I found myself sliding free. This time, instead of a dangerous eye, I was greeted by a deluge of blood and viscous fluid seeping from where its eye had been. My hair stuck to it, my clothes were soaked in it, but I shoved my disgust away. Resting my knee along the edge of the orbital socket, I used the leverage to push myself up. As soon as I had a strong launching point, I summoned another ice dagger into my hand and jumped at its other eye.

I'd mistimed my leap, or the basilisk moved at just the wrong moment, but I skidded down the middle of its face and nearly missed my target. Its attempt to snap me out of the air gave me a second chance. As it opened its mouth, it pushed me up, and I stabbed the dagger into its other eye.

Blinded and angry, the basilisk doubled its efforts to come after me, but I was already tumbling off its face. I landed on the ground with a loud "Oomph" as my breath was knocked from my lungs, and Adrian stepped in with the opportunity I'd left him to slice through the basilisk's throat.

The creature collapsed to the ground and curled in on itself, the colour of its scales lightening in the dim moonlight and crumbling until its remains were nothing more than dozens of extra boulders littering the valley.

I rose on shaking legs and, in an act of futility, tried to wipe the blood and muck off my breeches and shirt. I didn't want to think about the state of my hair.

Adrian wiped his blades with a clean cloth before sheathing them, tore one of the sharp fangs from the basilisk's stony corpse, and approached me with a toothy grin. The moonlight shining through the trees glinted off his marble skin and white teeth.

"Well done, mia Katerina," he said, handing me the fang. "We'll make a hunter of you yet."

From then on, Adrian never left me at home when he went hunting. As soon as word reached him of some new threat, we set out.

His greatest complaint was our limit in how far we could go, never anywhere that took more than a few days to travel. Any farther than that and the creature was often gone by the time we arrived.

"One day there will be faster modes of transportation," he grumbled. "Until then, only our closest neighbours can benefit from our guilt-ridden attempts to keep the world safe."

When Emrick returned after three weeks away, Adrian filled him in on our adventures, and although he wasn't thrilled about my participation, he didn't say anything to argue against it. Maybe he trusted my ability to take care of myself, but more likely he trusted his friend to ensure I didn't do anything too foolish.

Little did he know, Adrian encouraged all my foolish ideas, and they often worked.

Nymphs, spirits, demons—there was nothing Adrian wasn't willing to face, and thanks to him, I learned more about what existed in the world in the next seven years than I had in twenty-four with my family.

When I wasn't fighting, I was studying, not only my magic, but the texts Adrian had written documenting his knowledge and experience about the creatures he faced. In the evenings, while we danced in the hall, he quizzed me on what I'd learned. During battle, he would shout questions at me, challenging me to remember details about our enemy's strengths and weaknesses. Not only did I learn quickly, it being a matter of life and pain, but the back and forth often threw off our quarry, leaving them open to attacks they might have otherwise guarded against.

Adrian lived by his basic hunting rules: never hunt out in

the open, only target supernaturals who upset the balance, and always carry an extra knife.

Simple and to the point, but they'd never let him down.

Though I quickly began to wonder if the reason for his casual rules wasn't overconfidence but a readiness, or maybe an eagerness, to fail.

I watched him throw himself into the most dangerous situations without pause or reflection. No enemy was too strong or too numerous, and although he gave his all to win—or so it appeared—his lack of caring struck me as downright suicidal.

After each victory, he would clean his blades, shrug, and tell me to prepare for the next, never celebrating or acknowledging the fight beyond his sense of satisfaction or congratulating me for some skill or feat of prowess I'd demonstrated.

After years of noticing this same pattern, I finally worked up the courage to ask him about it.

We'd recently returned home following an intense battle against a giant in the Dolomites, and Adrian was in a fine mood. When I asked my question, he chuckled and walked me through the hops and skips of a dance. "Ah, cuore mio, after so many centuries, I invite Death. While I remain on this earth, I will do whatever I can to make up for the damage I've caused, but when the day comes that I can leave it behind me, I will happily do so. It makes me fearless in battle. Never reckless—I will always fight to win if it means my enemy is vanquished and can do no more harm—but willing to do whatever it takes without worrying about the consequences. Liberating, empowering, and exhilarating."

"Nothing you should be chasing, Kate," Emrick spoke up from where he'd appeared against the wall.

I shot him a look that dared him to try and stop me if the whim took me.

Adrian took my hand and spun me in a wide circle. "I must confess, though, that battling giants has begun to lose its thrill. I'm not sure what I'll do when I stop enjoying it."

"Lock yourself in your library listening to the latest songs and drinking vintage blood, I'm sure," Emrick said.

Adrian groaned. "If that day comes, kill me yourself, old friend. Don't let me languish in this world with no better way to spend my time than by spending time."

The song ended, but instead of excusing the players as he usually did, Adrian took my hand, escorted me to Emrick, and gestured for the musicians to take up their instruments again.

"Katerina needs more practice, and I need to feed. Indulge me, won't you, Emrick?"

He didn't wait for Emrick to respond before he left the hall, leaving the two of us standing there, our hands together, bare palm to gloved one, music filling the space with its cheery tune.

I stared at our connected hands, feeling all the awkwardness of a young woman unfamiliar with a man's touch—nervous, excited, afraid of rejection but equally terrified of acceptance.

Wanting to put us both out of our misery, I made to pull away, but to my surprise, Emrick curled his fingers through mine and held fast.

I raised my gaze to his and found him staring at me with firm resolution written in the set of his jaw.

He stepped away from the wall, walking me backwards to the middle of the floor. When he bent into a low bow, I dropped into a stunned curtsy. Emrick had never danced with me before. Usually he disappeared when Adrian summoned the musicians, leaving us to our "base human entertainment" as he referred to it.

But as we flowed through the dance, he took every step, skip, and turn with such easy grace that I might have believed he practiced when we weren't around.

Not once did he look away from me. I knew this for a fact because I kept my eyes fixed on him to see if he did.

The tension in the air was palpable. Not negative, not uncomfortable, but thick with unspoken words. The silver ring of his eyes around the deep blackness, the way his palm pressed fully against mine…

My heart kept beat with the skipping rhythm, and my stomach fluttered.

I imagined rising on tiptoe to kiss him, his arm wrapping

around my waist to hold me closer, a low growl rising from his throat as he gave in to whatever need drove him to stand so close to me in the garden or to lead me in this dance.

I also imagined rising on tiptoe to kiss him, him pulling back, startled, disgusted, and having to spend eternity with that mortification hanging over me.

The confusion left me dizzy, and I tripped on the next turn, nearly winding up face first on the stone floor if Emrick hadn't caught my arm to steady me.

"I'm sorry," I said before he could ask if I was all right. "I must be tired. Excuse me."

I pulled my hand free and hurried out of the room, aware only of Emrick staring after me until I was gone.

22

Emrick

Florence, Italy - April 1223

I WATCHED KATERINA leave, swallowing the urge to call after her and ask what had happened. It was better that she left. I had no idea what had pushed me to dance with her in the first place.

Adrian had passed me her hand, and I hadn't been able to let go even as my lips had formed my apologies. Instead of wishing her a good night, I'd gone through the steps I'd watched other people take hundreds of times as though I'd danced them myself every night. She made it easy to pretend I had.

The warmth of her palm through my glove, taunting me with its closeness, the flush of her skin as her pulse raced, the darkening of her eyes as she'd looked at me, never once shifting her focus to anything else, had driven me to the edge of madness, and I'd found myself longing to kiss her.

Then she'd run, and I remained frozen in the hall, unable to go after her, unwilling to carry on as though nothing had happened.

The players fell silent, and I dismissed them for the night before finally taking myself outside to the garden. The sweet-scented air, thick with coming rain, brushed against my lips and soothed my senses. I closed my eyes to appreciate the peace of the hour.

"Finished already?" Adrian asked, stepping out of the shadows.

I shot him a narrowed look. "You should be surprised I started at all."

He chuckled and gestured for me to walk with him. I fell into step beside him, and we wandered through his precious garden to the stone benches in the pavilion.

"Ah, my friend," he sighed as he sat down. "Do you know, it's been four hundred years since we met, and never in that time have I seen you happy? Forgive me if I'm trying to change that."

"By pushing me to dance? If so, then in four hundred years, you haven't learned much about me."

Adrian scoffed. "If I were attracted to the female sex, you'd be at risk of me stealing her away from you, Emrick. Here is this woman, beautiful, intelligent, kind, driven—immortal. And bound to you."

"Against her will," I reminded him. "In an act of betrayal at the expense of her family. That sort of trauma stays with you, no matter how many years pass."

"As you well know."

My friend's knowing stare bored into me, and I ignored it. He was trying to get me to talk about Gabrielle, the woman who'd promised me forever then turned away when I'd offered it. I wasn't going to lie that Katerina had brought up many memories of my late wife, but Gaby wasn't what held me back.

Kate's life was bound to mine, but not by any bargaining on her part. Not by any promises she had no intention of keeping. She was stuck here, just as I was, something that put us on more even ground than anyone else I'd encountered in my five hundred years, Adrian excepted.

"I am Death, Adrian. Or as good as." I cupped the back of my neck and rested my knee on the bench beside where he sat. "You don't believe she deserves better than someone who spends most of his time escorting magic users into the after-life? She has the possibility of *living* her extended years. You have a better chance of offering her that, regardless of your inclinations, than I do."

Adrian pursed his lips, and I recognized the expression as his attempt to hide a smile. "So you'll admit you've considered it."

"Of course I've considered it. I'm not insensible."

The memory of her dancing around the bonfire on the night I met her pressed behind my eyelids, and I closed my eyes to savour it. Her black hair long and loose, flying out behind her as she spun in circles with a younger woman I now knew had been her sister. The way she'd exposed her throat as she laughed, the sparkle in her eyes as she enjoyed the life she'd been born to.

Even then, I'd seen her longing to be more than she was—though I'd had no idea at the time that her wishes included hunting magical beasts—but all such desire had disappeared when someone had handed a young boy into her arms. On him, she'd delivered a hundred tiny kisses until he'd shrieked with delight, and then they were both off, spinning and dancing away until the night grew dark and the betrayers had begun their wicked ritual.

I came out of the memory to find Adrian watching me, not even bothering to hide his smile now.

"All I'm saying is you should think about it, Emrick. The poor girl is only seventy-five years into her immortality. She has no idea of the loneliness awaiting her. As the language, the fashion, the borders change, and she must constantly struggle to keep up if she doesn't want to be left behind and eventually become a threat someone like me has to deal with. As everything that was once familiar fades into the past and all that's left are the fading memories that pale with each review. Sanity becomes a challenge if one doesn't have purpose. Connection. *Passion.*"

"You could provide two out of three at least. And no end of dancing."

"I could indeed, and I intend to. I've come to care for her deeply. Fiercely, even. Her company has rejuvenated my enjoyment of everything I once held dear, and if you would give yourself the chance, she might do the same for you."

Or I might destroy her and be trapped for eternity with the knowledge that I'd ruined the best thing to happen to me in centuries.

Adrian chuckled and rose to his feet. "I will not push, and I will not play games with either of your hearts. Neither of you would forgive me for it. All I suggest is you take whatever opportunity you can to dance with her. One never knows what might evolve from a simple touch."

23

Katerina

Black Forest, Germany - August 1223

Four months later, Adrian and I were on our way to the Northern Black Forest.

It was the farthest we'd travelled for a hunt, but a vampire named Isabella, one of Adrian's old associates, had reached out for help as a personal favour, and Adrian hadn't been able to refuse.

An old nestmate of his had gone rogue, slaughtered enough of her kind to declare herself a queen, and was drinking the outskirts of the forest dry. Many villages had already been affected, vampire numbers were swelling, and they were attracting attention from the Church and nobility, neither of which boded well for the safety of the human beings who were simply trying to survive this blight and live their lives.

The cart moved quickly along the darkened roads, and I didn't bother to look farther than the horses' ears, certain my stomach would revolt if I attempted to take in the scenery.

Even after so long, I hadn't quite got the hang of rapid transportation.

It could also have been nerves.

For seven years I'd hunted with Adrian, honing my skills, learning my magic, and although I prided myself on the progress I'd made—including some new tricks I looked forward to putting into action—I wasn't cocky enough to think this mission wouldn't be a challenge. A whole nest of vampires against only me and Adrian? We worked well together, made a formidable team, but this would be like pitting myself against a high dragon instead of the smaller drakes we'd come across along the country's northern border.

"A vampire's greatest asset is their speed," Adrian said for the fifteenth time tonight. I knew well enough he was trying to hide his own nervousness by lecturing me on how best to defend myself. "They'll try to come at you from different angles, making it seem as though they're closing in on all sides at once, but they'll end up developing a predictable pattern in how they move. I've learned to avoid this by developing more of a herding strategy, but most of these vampires will be fledglings, so they'll run on instinct alone. Instinct and hunger. That will be where your advantage lies. They'll be ruthless, but they'll be single-minded. As long as you stay creative, you'll be able to get the better of them."

I covered his hand with mine and leaned in to press a kiss against his cool cheek. "I appreciate your advice, Adrian. No one could teach me these things better than you."

He huffed and turned his hand over so our fingers intertwined. "It was my decision to bring you into these battles, and I know now I couldn't stop you if I wanted to, but fights like this make me wish I'd convinced you to stay home. Your existence on this earth is too precious to waste, mia Katerina."

I squeezed his hand and enjoyed the surge of warmth around my heart. Never would I have imagined the friendship of a vampire would come to mean so much to me. "My life is only worth what I'm able to give back. That's what I was raised hearing, and it's the motto I've sworn to live by. My place is by your side and nowhere else."

Adrian replied with a low chuckle. "That might be true for now, tesoro, but perhaps not forever. Life has a funny way of making people see their true priorities."

I stared at him, waiting for him to explain, but he shook his head and flicked the horse's reins, still wearing that smile that told me he was enjoying some secret amusement at my expense.

Not much later, as we sped through the dark wood, the horses whinnied and the cart lurched hard enough that I tumbled from the seat into the wagon behind me. Adrian landed on top of me, covering me as something wrenched off the wooden gate at the back of the wagon and threw it aside.

Shrieks and hisses pierced my ears, and I tucked my chin to my chest the way Adrian had taught me. Anything to make a vampire's target harder to access. With Adrian so close, I couldn't summon my fire without hurting him, which left me vulnerable with only the knife in my pocket to protect me.

"Remember, Katerina," he whispered in my ear, "use their instincts against them."

Then he was gone, out of the cart and out of sight, as were the vampires that had stopped us.

I leapt out of the wagon and immediately brought fire into my hands, lighting up the woods with the flame. It was a dangerous move, as I'd turned myself into a beacon to gain their attention, but it also served as a warning to them not to come closer. Vampires burned, and the older they were, the faster they turned to ash.

But Adrian was right—if I wanted to ensure my safety, I had to use every tool in my arsenal. While being drained might not kill me, I wasn't likely to come back if someone tore off my head.

Air brushed my skin from behind, and I lashed out my

flame like a whip, striking the creature trying to sneak up behind me and wrapping it around her throat. She bared her fangs and hissed, then reached for the whip only to find her fingers caught by the fire.

I left her to the flames as two more vampires came in from the front and beside me. Both of them were pale and beautiful in the moonlight, their perfect features sharp and alluring. All the better to draw in their prey and convince them it was in their best interest to lay down their lives as dinner.

But I had no interest in being someone's meal. I drew more fire into my hands and spun in a circle, letting the flame stretch around me until it formed a sphere of light and heat. Both vampires backed off but didn't flee, watching me closely for any sign of faltering. They intended to wait me out, and as more vampires snuck in from the trees, I knew my time was limited. They had until the sun rose to bring me down; I had until my magic waned.

I had a better idea of my abilities than they did, however, so I held on to the power surging through me, keeping it contained. I waited until they crept closer, a dozen of them coming in from all sides. Did they plan to share me amongst the twelve, or would they fight between themselves until the winner claimed the feast?

Unfortunate for them that none would be alive to enjoy it.

With my heart racing, praying my idea worked, I shoved

outwards and sent the fire flying in the circle I'd formed. It sliced through the twelve vampires, consuming them, leaving me free to run through the woods in search of Adrian.

I stumbled to a stop when I cleared the trees to find my friend locked in battle with another six vampires. He was faster, but they were many, and although his darting around did seem to have worked in guiding them all to the centre of the small clearing, I wasn't sure how he thought to dominate them.

Of course I should have put faith in my friend. I watched in surprise and no small degree of admiration as he herded them beneath a large oak. In another heartbeat, he'd climbed the tree, and the branch overhead, at least as wide around as I was, cracked and fell on them, crushing the six beneath its weight. From there, it was a simple matter for him to slice his nails through their necks, and in another blink, they'd met their final death.

He looked up, winked at me, and disappeared again, leaving me to chase after him on my slower human legs.

The deeper we ran into the forest, the more hisses and jeers taunted me. They had to be everywhere, dozens if not hundreds of vampires swarming, cutting us off from each other and the edges of the woods. What were they all doing here?

And where was Adrian's contact—the one who'd asked us for help?

There was no way the two of us could fend off so many.

Unless I wanted to burn the entire Black Forest to the ground, I had to be careful with my fire, so I summoned my ice and formed two stakes that I held tight, visible enough for my enemy to see I was armed. I doubted it would do much to hold off their attacks, but I hoped it might give them pause while they rethought their approach.

A sudden drop in temperature and movement at my side made me jump with a stifled shriek, and I raised an ice stake only to have a warm, gloved hand close around my wrist. I looked up with wide eyes and met Emrick's moonlight stare. My racing heart skipped a beat as my breath caught in my throat.

"What are you doing here?" I asked, keeping my voice low. I hadn't seen him since our interrupted dance so many months ago. For him to appear out of the mist was more than a small shock to my fight-addled mind.

"Helping you get out of this predicament with most of your blood still inside your body."

Under his gaze, my mouth went dry. Then he shifted to put his back to mine, and I craned my neck to keep him in view. "What happened to *not getting involved?*"

He shrugged. "They're vampires. They're already dead. No conflict of interest."

That was the only explanation I got before the vampires charged. Adrian had long disappeared from view, but the sounds of fighting reached us from farther in the woods. I sent out a wish that he would find his way to us, then turned my attention to the ten vampires bearing down on me.

They moved so fast I couldn't track them. Sharp nails sliced along my cheek, and more clawed at my breeches, cutting through to my thigh. The scent of blood filled my nose, and the vampires responded with hungry shrieks as more spilled through the trees. A leather glove flew past my line of vision, and I caught sight of Emrick's bare hand before he reached out to grab a vampire from the air. At his touch, the man crumbled to ash, the first time I'd witnessed Emrick's ability since the wolf attack so many decades ago.

The sight of the vampire flaking away made my thoughts stutter, and my hands dropped to my sides. For a flash, I was back in Palonia on the night Emrick and I had met, remembering the way he'd revealed himself by resting his hand on the corpse of one of my people.

Pain cut through me, emotional followed by physical as a vampire took advantage of my distraction to grab me and sink their teeth into my neck.

"Kate!"

Emrick tried to reach me, but four vampires latched on to him, tearing at his clothes, careful to avoid contact with his skin.

A second vampire approached as the other feasted behind me. Pain burst into pleasure as his venom spread, and my will to fight faded. So much easier to give in, let them take what they wanted.

A small corner of my mind remained my own, and I grabbed hold of it. When the vampire in front of me came close enough, her starving gaze focused on the other side of my neck, I tightened my grip on one of the ice stakes and drove it into her chest. She bared her teeth before bursting into ash. Riding the rush of my kill, I threw my elbow into the gut of the vampire behind me. He grunted, and his grip on me loosened, giving me a good enough angle to wrap my hand around his wrist. With a surge of power, I dragged my fire through the ice and set him alight. He released me long enough to try to run, not realizing the heat came from himself. In a flash of flame that was there and gone, he disintegrated.

More vampires lurked among the trees, far enough in the shadows that I couldn't make out how many. I sprinted towards them, pulling back my heat and forming a dozen spikes of ice that I launched outwards. Three struck home. One must have pierced a heart, because a cloud of ash rose to my left. A second vampire thrashed against a tree trunk, impaled through the shoulder, and a third slowed enough for me to see her as she ran towards me with a spike through her leg. I switched back to fire as she came close, spreading it over my hands, and although she tried to detour at the last moment, she was too late. I grabbed her face, and her screams filled the night until she was silent.

My pulse throbbed in my ears, and I tasted blood at the back of my throat as I heaved for breath. My focus on the battle had turned my vision to pinpricks, and lights flashed in my periphery. Fear or fatigue, I didn't know, but either way I couldn't stop. Not with so many monsters still out there waiting for me to falter.

"There are too many," Emrick said as he reached my side. His bare hands were raised, ready to touch anyone who came too close. "What were you two thinking coming out here on your own?"

I scowled and scanned the treeline, fire licking my palms and creeping over my gloves. "That we'd have time to join Adrian's reinforcements before the fight."

"What reinforcements, Kate? These *are* the reinforcements."

I stumbled and turned to look at him. "What are you talking about? Adrian's friend asked us to come here and help them deal with a problem."

We were separated as four more vampires darted out of the trees. Dredging up my energy, I threw more ice spikes. I was learning how to notice the faint shimmer in the air that marked where a vampire was moving, and my aim landed true as ash rained over the thick grass.

Another snuck around me and nearly got its fangs in my

neck, but I spun at the last moment, summoned my fire, and spread my palm over their face. Their fang nicked my finger, and their expression was one of confusion as they caught a drop of blood the moment before they burst.

"The problem they're dealing with," Emrick continued as though we hadn't been interrupted, "is Adrian."

More vampires came. I summoned two ice stakes and drove one into the chest of a woman launching herself at me.

"Excuse me?"

I spun, ducked beneath the arms of a vampire trying to grab me, and came up behind her to stab her through the back with my second one.

"Our friend has made a name for himself throughout Europe." Emrick threw himself forward and grabbed a vampire by the arm as I wheeled behind him and flung a handful of spikes towards three charging women. One went down right away, the other two slowed long enough for Emrick and I to split the kills. "He's become known as a menace to supernatural kind. The queen, Isabella, doesn't agree with this *balance* he's trying to set."

The old friend who had contacted Adrian *was* the rogue queen?

And we'd walked right into her trap.

As I turned again, my shock and fury morphed into exhausted frustration as five more vampires spilled into the clearing. Emrick was right. There were too many.

"What would she prefer?" I asked as I struggled to draw more ice spikes into my palms. "That we reveal ourselves to the world? Because I'm sure that would go over well."

My aim slipped, and all but one spike missed their targets. Three of the vampires came for me, while the other two misjudged and targeted Emrick. They disintegrated the moment they leapt at him, but by then I was on the ground, one vampire sinking her fangs into my arm, a second into my neck, a third into my leg. Sharp pain made me cry out, but my fear turned to rage as I pumped fire through my blood.

Emrick grabbed the one on my leg by the neck at the same time my fire consumed the other two, and in another heartbeat, corpse ash rained on me.

My stomach turned, and I rolled onto my side to catch my breath.

For a blessed moment, we were alone in the clearing, though by the sounds reaching us through the trees, Adrian was still fighting.

A cry sounded, a familiar voice, and Emrick and I exchanged a wide-eyed glance.

"Go," I said, and he hesitated only a moment before stepping into the mist and disappearing.

I rose to my feet, shook out my arms to work feeling back into my fingers, and started after him.

In the momentary silence, my earlier fury at Isabella sparked through me, and I clenched my hands around the fire that threatened to spread up my arms.

I was done tolerating betrayals. These vampires had wiped out villages and instilled fear into people who didn't understand what was happening, but for me, this queen's greatest crime was lying to a man who trusted her.

She might have planned tonight to be our end, but I would not go down until I took every last one of her nest with me.

If only I could find Emrick and Adrian. Somewhere in the trees, I'd lost track of the noise. It came from all around me, branches snapping, hisses, cries. The air was thick with the stench of smoke and ash. My senses were so overwhelmed, my muscles so weighed down with fatigue, that I couldn't get my bearings, and before long, I found myself lost on the edge of a valley, unsure which way to go.

A chuckle sounded through the trees, coming from all directions, and I turned in a circle, braced for attack.

"What is this tasty morsel my old friend has brought me?" The voice was alluring. Deep but most certainly female.

I spun around. Thick fog had crept across the ground from between the trees, blocking my view of anything beyond where I stood. The sounds of fighting from beyond dulled, the moonlight above grew brighter as the leaves seemed to shift overhead, and a woman stepped out of the shadows.

Her hair was as black as mine, partly pulled into a knot on top of her head while the rest hung thick and loose around her shoulders. Her skin was corpse-pale across sharp, delicate features, her lips painted a deep red—or perhaps tinted by a recent meal. A black gown hugged her chest and waist before pooling in an obsidian waterfall over her hips to the ground.

She looked as dangerous as any untrained noblewoman I'd met, but the power that wafted off her made my mouth go dry.

"I'm so pleased Adrian accepted our invitation," she said.

As my heart raced, she smirked and raised a hand towards me. "Well then, my dear, aren't you going to greet me properly? In this world, you bow to a vampire queen."

Fear flared in my chest. This was Isabella? Her power made the rest of the monsters we'd fought tonight look like kittens.

Yet here I was, exhausted, drained, needing to face her.

And I was alone.

24

Katerina

Black Forest, Germany - August 1223

I DIDN'T BOW.

I didn't waste any time, hoping that if I moved quickly enough, I might catch her off guard.

With no thought for the trees and worried only for my future, I threw out a blast of fire, but at my first move, she vanished, and I wheeled around in a quick circle to try to track her.

Unlike the younger vampires, she left no shimmer in the air, either moving too quickly or absorbing herself into the fog to travel unseen. Not every vampire possessed that skill, but queens didn't claim their position by democratic vote—they earned it through violence and power. I'd learned this through Adrian's many tomes on the subject and wished now I'd paid more attention to what those skills might be.

"I smell you, *sorceress*." Isabella's voice drifted on the air, a taunting, teasing lure. "It's been a long time since I've tasted one of your kind."

I drew new ice stakes into my palms and continued to turn in slow circles, searching for any sign of where she might be. But there was only a whoosh of air as she swept past me, and I slapped my hand over my neck at the pinprick of pain that was there and gone.

A moment of silence, then a hiss that scraped the insides of my ears. "What is this magic? You are a sorceress, yet like nothing I've tasted before. Magic and death, life and decay. How is this possible?"

I didn't bother to reply. This vampire didn't deserve any answers about who or what I was.

A branch snapped behind me, and I threw out a handful of ice spikes. They soared towards the woman's shadow, but none struck as Isabella exploded into a cloud of bats that beat their tiny wings past my head, blocking my view of the valley, the fog, the moon with the sheer number of them. Their tiny screeches and the rustle of wingbeats made it impossible to hear anything else. I clapped my hands over my ears and crouched low to avoid them, and a ringing laughter echoed through my head.

When I looked up again, the bats were coalescing on top of the hill, reforming into the queen. Isabella used her thumb to brush a spot of blood from the corner of her lip. "I'd hoped to get my fill tonight, but it seems my old friend keeps strange, unappetizing company these days. A shame for you, my dear. As intriguing as you are, I now have no reason to be gentle with you."

She bared her teeth and rushed me. I attempted to leap out of her way, but a blow landed in my gut as she passed me, and I doubled over, wrapping my arms around my stomach. I didn't have time to catch my breath before she swept by me again, this time with a strike to my temple that sent me to the ground. In a flicker, she reappeared and wrapped her hand around my throat to pin me beneath her.

"I'll be sure to tell Adrian how you died begging for your life. It will cause him such wonderful agony to know he was the cause of it."

She grinned, and the pressure on my neck increased as she prepared to snap it. I doubted the broken neck would kill me, but it would slow me down. And if she ripped my head from my shoulders, I was finished.

Panic filled me, and I pumped fire through my blood so quickly I didn't have time to prepare for it. Her skin sizzled against mine, and I cried out at the shock of pain. Isabella lurched away, and I rolled onto my hands and knees, doing my best to push myself to my feet on shaking legs. My ribs screamed at me, more than one undoubtedly cracked, and I tasted blood. With every breath, a sharp burn sliced through my middle, and I struggled to rise to my full height.

I drew my lingering magic around me and settled the fire against my skin, wrapping myself in it so she couldn't grab me again. My clothes burned away, leaving me dressed only in the dancing flames and my runed gloves. Although the fire would do nothing to take Isabella down unless I successfully made and maintained contact, it gave me a much needed moment to heal.

My ribs snapped back into place, each shift of bone and organ, every inch of sealing tissue making me clench my teeth to avoid screaming, but I wouldn't give her the satisfaction of hearing my torment. The small amount of healing wasn't enough, not nearly, but full recovery from the damage I'd taken would take hours. At least for now I was on my feet.

Somewhere out there, Adrian and Emrick still had to be fighting, and as long as they were busy, I would keep Isabella focused on me. Emrick would be safe enough, but I didn't trust her not to rip out Adrian's heart. If I could keep her distracted until they wiped out her nest and were able to join me, we could work together to destroy her.

With that goal in mind, I absorbed my fire, allowed frost to cover my body in a layer of icy armour, and launched a dozen ice spikes in every direction. Most of them struck the shadows beyond the fog, but one must have landed. Her hiss rattled my skull, and when she appeared again on top of the low hill, her dress was torn at the sleeve and blood dripped down her arm.

"No one has marred my flesh in centuries, little sorceress," she said, her fangs fully extended, so much longer than Adrian's despite his age. "You will pay for this."

She vanished and again came the bats. This time, instead of swooping over me, they caged me, fluttering, biting, scratching. Hundreds of them taking pinches out of my flesh.

By the time they flew off, my frost armour was nothing more than patches, and I was missing chunks of skin from my arms, legs, and torso. Between the larger wounds were thousands of smaller punctures, each one weeping blood.

My head swam. I staggered on my feet but caught myself before I fell. I had to stay conscious or she would win, and I found myself fighting hard against that possibility. The thought of not having a chance to say goodbye to Adrian or Emrick, the thought that I might die while this evil creature lived to take so many more lives, simmered deep in my soul. I wouldn't allow it to happen.

I was done playing games. She wanted to test my limits? She wanted to know what I was?

Let her find out.

I sought the stillness, not bothering to breathe or find my

grounding. It turned out Emrick was right—I couldn't waste the time.

The bats settled, and a chuckle rumbled around me, making my stomach flutter with its tantalizing note. Isabella appeared in front of me. And beside me. And on my other side. In a series of smoke puffs, a dozen Isabellas encircled me. Illusions made of mist with only one true queen, or had she divided herself into multiple forms?

If I survived this, I would need to ask Adrian and pay far more attention to my studies.

Refusing to be distracted, I redoubled my focus on the magic surging within me. My power felt prickly, unfamiliar, and the temptation was strong to release it and grab the more comfortable fire that lurked so close to the surface. Instead, I tightened my grip on it, pooling it within me while restraining it, wanting to make sure my hold was firm before I let go.

"Give up, girl," Isabella said. "Your friends aren't coming. For as many of my children as they kill, I'll send a hundred more. This is my domain—these are my woods. If anyone walks out of here, it's because I wish it, and what I want now, more than anything, is to wipe the taste of you from my mouth and make Adrian suffer for bringing you to me in the first place."

She bared her teeth at me, but I wasn't listening.

Sparks jumped between my fingers, and my hands twitched under the force of it. My breath quickened, my heart raced, and I stretched my arms out at my sides. The unfamiliar magic coiled tightly within me, begging to be released.

She laughed again. "Is this where you impress me with a light show? Believe me, my dear, I've seen all your kind has to offer. I've drunk so many sorcerers dry, this country is rid of them. You're a dying breed, a species racing towards extinction. Only we immortals will endure. Only we immortals will rule."

Through the blood dripping down my face, I smiled. "I suppose only one of us will be around to see if you're right. Unfortunately, Your Majesty, it won't be you."

Before she had time to voice her confusion or her ridicule, I let go of the lightning within me. A buzz scurried through my veins as arcs flew from my palms, splitting into multiple streams that bounced across the clearing into the chests of each form of the vampire queen.

I was the bubble that had burst, the storm that had struck. As the energy within me poured out in a deluge, I sank into the hum and embraced the flow of power.

When the magic hit the original, the illusions vanished, and the lightning struck the trees instead. Fire swept upwards through their branches, lighting the night sky with a glow that would call every nocturnal supernatural across the country, but there was nothing for it.

Ash rained down over the clearing as Isabella dropped to her knees. Fire spread across her gown and over her aged flesh.

It swept over her face, and her screams reached me beyond the roar of the flames.

My magic drained, the threat extinguished, I collapsed to the ground. A chill ran through me that no amount of closing in on myself could reach. The trembling began in my hands, but as quickly as the fire had consumed Isabella, it took over the rest of my body, leaving me a quaking mess on the valley floor.

Only vaguely was I aware of voices coming closer, of gentle arms wrapping around me.

"The cart—" Adrian said.

"My way is faster," Emrick replied.

White mist enveloped me, and the last I saw of the forest was the reflection of the fire catching the fine droplets of the gateway that led to the afterlife. Light against darkness; life against death; passion against coldness. A chuckle rumbled through me, but before I had time to voice my thoughts, sleep claimed me, and I drifted off in Emrick's arms.

25

Katerina

Florence, Italy - August 1223

I AWOKE WARM, snuggled deep beneath wool blankets. I had no idea how long I'd slept, but by how rested I felt, I suspected it might have been days.

Light that had become familiar over the years shone through the open balcony beside my bed, and I knew I was back at Adrian's estate.

Alive when a vampire queen was dead.

Because I had killed her.

I, Katerina of Palonia, who had never been considered a useful member of my community thanks to my inability to harness my magic, had defeated an ancient being all on my own.

No small amount of pride swelled in my chest, and I threw my arms over my head with a groan of satisfaction as my muscles stretched. No pain accompanied the gesture beyond a slight stiffness in my joints. Curious, I threw back the blankets, but all that met my eye was a stretch of smooth, pale skin. Not even a bruise remained from my encounter with the queen, only the scars and markings that had existed at the time of my binding.

I traced my fingers over the knots that made up the dragon tattoo along my right thigh and thought of my parents. Would they have been proud of me for my victory? Would they have turned to the teachers who'd said I wouldn't amount to anything and pointed out how wrong they'd been? Or would they not be at all surprised, having known it was inevitable that I would find someone to help me break through the barriers that held me back?

My heart ached that I would never know for sure, that any answer I came up with was speculation based on experience, and I wondered when I would stop searching for their approval. Centuries? Millennia? Until the day the tether between Emrick and I snapped and I was free to join them?

The coldness of grief chased away the heat of contentment, and I hurried to get out of bed and throw on the simple woollen shift lying on the chair. At some point Natalia would be here to help me get dressed, but for the time being, I settled for comfort and made my way to the garden.

Based on the angle of the sun, it was only mid-morning, which meant hours before Adrian woke up to fill me in on everything that had happened while I fought Isabella. I settled myself on a stone bench and watched the dappled sunlight dance across the flowers. A soft breeze set the stems swaying, and in their movement, I was brought back to memories of the hall, of musicians playing a merry tune as a gloved hand walked me through a series of kicks and spins.

As though my thought of Emrick had summoned him, he stepped out of the afterlife into the garden beside me. He was dressed as he usually was—hide breeches secured by a thick leather belt, unbleached linen shirt unlaced at the chest so a hint of his wolf tattoo showed underneath, blond hair tied back, gloves on.

He didn't meet my gaze, his attention focused on the flowers, and a deep furrow lined the space between his eyebrows.

"I didn't think you'd be awake for a while yet," he said. "It was a long night."

I raised my eyebrows. "One night? I could have sworn it was longer. So is Adrian not home yet?"

Emrick rested his knee on the bench beside me. "He's still in Germany, holed up in one of his safe houses. It'll take him a few days to return."

He still hadn't looked at me, and I wondered what was on

his mind. Why had he come here if he didn't want to see me? Had his thoughts also returned to our dance? That moment between us before I'd panicked and fled?

Heat warmed my cheeks, and I averted my gaze to join his intense scrutiny of the garden. "Thanks for letting me know. I'll make sure I don't burn the place down in his absence."

The comment earned me a faint smile. "As long as the story's good, he probably wouldn't care if you did. He'd say it was time for him to move on anyway."

I tipped my head, acknowledging the point. I'd been here for fourteen years, and Adrian had been here for three before that. From what he'd told me of his patterns, it was long past time he packed up and recreated his life.

Too bad, really. I would miss this wonderful breeze and these beautiful gardens. Unless he meant for me to stay here. Alone.

My heart lurched at the thought of being left behind. "Do you think he'll let me go with him when he leaves?"

Emrick chuckled. "I don't think you could escape him now if you wanted to. He sees you as one of his own. A thrall without the magical binding."

I smirked. "You mean a friend?"

"As much as he's capable of having one of those, yes."

"What about you?"

I didn't know what prompted me to ask the question. The

warmth of the sun on my skin, the sweetness of the wind, the brightness of the flowers, or the flush of victory. I had defeated a vampire queen with a new and latent magic. My skin hummed with the lingering rush of that fight, giving me the courage to meet Emrick's eye as he finally looked my way.

"What about me?" he asked.

"Are you capable of having friends?"

His smile turned dry. "Is that what we are, Katerina?"

I shrugged, though my heart was making a valiant effort to beat its way past my ribs. "Maybe not. Perhaps we're doomed to be bound for eternity without ever moving beyond acquaintances and occasional fighting partners."

"Or occasional dancing partners," he offered.

I might have thought he was opening the way to talk about what happened if not for the faint flinch when he heard what he'd said. As usual, I opted to show mercy and settled on a nod. "Can't forget that."

Despite the light tone I was determined to keep, I couldn't fight the disappointment that tugged down the hopes awakened by his question. Silly Katerina. What had I hoped for, exactly? An admission that the desire I'd seen in his eyes while we danced hadn't been all in my head? A passionate declaration of intent?

The thought nearly pushed me to laugh aloud, and I knew I had to remove myself from this conversation if I didn't want to embarrass myself.

I was suffering a temporary attraction, that was all. A few more decades in his company, and my feelings would fade into a distant appreciation of his good looks and confident demeanour. My stomach would stop fluttering whenever he showed up, my body would stop warming with longing for his returned interest.

Resolved, I stood to leave. "I should get back to my rooms before Natalia discovers I went out in such scandalous attire. She's lectured me often enough about my lack of propriety that I think she enjoys it. Gives her something to talk about other than Adrian's bizarre feeding habits." I inclined my head towards him. "I'll see you later."

I started back to the estate, but at his quiet, "Wait," I stopped and turned back—only to find him close behind me. He'd moved so silently I hadn't heard him.

I tilted my head back to look into his eyes, noted that the furrow had returned between his eyebrows, and ordered my pulse to slow down. It didn't listen.

"Last night…" he began, then stopped and ran his fingers through his hair. His eyes grew darker, clouds over the moon. "I was supposed to stay with you. You're the reason I was there in the first place, to make sure you were all right once I realized where Adrian had gone. But I left you alone to face Isabella, and I'm sorry."

I pulled at a loose thread on my skirt. "You left to help Adrian. I would never resent you for that."

His gloved hand reached for mine, and my traitorous heart leapt at the contact, only beating faster as he stroked his thumb over the backs of my fingers.

For a moment, he seemed to battle with himself, but just as I was certain he would disappear again, he squeezed my hand and said, "Adrian is important to me, yes, but you… You ask if we're friends, Kate? No. I would never use that word to describe what we are." At my inquiring look, he continued, "From the moment those sorceresses cast that spell, your life was bound to mine, but my *everything* was bound to you. You carry my heart and what's left of my soul. You make me see there's still life in this world worth valuing. When I'm with you, I'm more than just a face of Death. I feel like myself again."

I dipped my head to hide the blush that spread across my cheeks. I was a hundred years old, for goodness' sake, not some sentimental young woman experiencing romance for the first time. Yet his words reached deep inside me and awoke something I'd begun to think was dead and buried—a vulnerable corner of my heart I was terrified to access.

"You could have left me in Palonia with my dead kin," I said to his chest. "You could have abandoned me any time between England and Montpellier. You could have let Shogaur burn me alive. I owe you my existence for every time you stayed. But more than any of that, you kept me grounded to this earth when I wanted it to swallow me whole. You kept me walking, kept me eating, kept me warm. And if none of that was enough, you let me reconnect with my people in a way I never imagined possible by helping me tap into my magic. You say I've claimed your heart and soul? Believe me when I say, you've claimed mine as well."

"Kate…" My name came out as a whisper on his perfect lips, and when he bent his head, my breath stopped.

Before his mouth met mine, he froze, squeezed his eyes shut, and pulled away.

"What is it?" I asked, refusing to let him go far. "Every time I see this desire in you, you run. Why?"

He sighed and took both my hands, holding them against his shirt so I felt the heartbeat rushing beneath my palms. "I'm afraid."

I ducked to catch his eye, and the silver was molten, filled with such conflicted anguish my insides twisted. "Of what?"

"Of touching you." The words came out as barely a breath. "Of getting close to someone who has changed my life in such a profound way only to lose you in my arms at the first contact."

"We've touched before."

I tried not to think of that night, but when the memories swept over me, they didn't stop me in pain as they'd done often enough in the past. For a change, the images at the forefront of my mind didn't focus on the corpses lying on the ground but on this man and how he'd been the morning after the massacre. Dressed the same as he was now with the addition of his fur-lined cloak, how he'd knelt beside the body of one of my teachers to return his flesh and bone to the earth.

How he'd begun to walk away, intending to leave me behind until I'd thrown myself at him and grabbed his arm. His bare arm.

The lurch in my stomach as I'd jumped through every moment of time and wound up standing exactly where I was, still whole.

"What if it was a mistake?" he asked, his voice rough with restrained emotion. "What if the spell was still fresh, guarding you from me? What if the next time we touch, you crumble to dirt? What would I do then? How could I continue without you now that I've tasted the world with you in it?"

Disappointment warred with compassion inside me. I wanted to grab him and kiss him regardless of his fears, but another part of me was drawn to soothe the torment blazing in his eyes. Desire against fear, passion against logic.

"What do you propose instead?" I asked. "That we feel these things and never act on them? Spend the next centuries circling each other, knowing what we want but not allowing ourselves to have it? Is that the life you see when you look at me?"

"No," he breathed, tightening his grip on my hand. Then he let go and stepped back. "But maybe it's for the best if that's all it is."

I pressed my lips together and nodded, refusing to let my tears fall as rejection and loneliness speared through me. "I would rather burn in a fire of passion than love for eternity without it. But if that's what you think best, then so be it. Perhaps it's enough to know the feelings exist."

It wasn't, not for me, but I wasn't about to force him into anything he didn't want. How would that benefit either of us?

I turned again, once more intending to return to my room, less interested now in Natalia's lecture but willing to endure it if it meant leaving this garden.

I hadn't taken three steps before Emrick's arm was around my waist. He turned me towards him and curled his other hand through my hair. "If you burn for this, I swear I'll find a way to follow."

He hesitated only a moment—to give me time to pull away, perhaps, or simply to work up his courage—before he bent his head and brushed his lips against mine.

Sparks burst under my skin from the crown of my head to the tips of my toes as the dust of my being was pulled through time only to land again in Adrian's garden. Emrick gasped against me, but I gave him no time to think or reconsider as I circled my arms around his neck and flattened my body against his. We'd tested his fears and proved them groundless. What was time to either of us?

He moaned against my mouth as our kiss deepened, and I held on as he drank me in, a man quenching his thirst after a drawn-out deprivation. No other kiss had ever clawed so deeply into my soul, latching on to and pulling out everything that made me human—weak and vulnerable, yet also strong and grounded.

He dragged his gloved hand across my cheek to brush my hair out of the way, chasing my lips with his, parting them with his tongue.

Desire welled hot and wet throughout my body, and a whimper crept out of my throat as I clung ever closer to him.

This was life. This was the beauty of having every pore aware and awake to the pleasures of passion. Shep had always been tender and gentle, but Emrick was all-consuming. Only a kiss, yet every other thought escaped my mind except him and this moment and the connection that bound us together.

"Take me to my room," I whispered against his mouth, and without moving us a step, Emrick wrapped us in mist and transported us to the floor beside my bed. Vaguely I was aware of the breakfast tray on the table where Natalia must have left it when she'd discovered me gone. The gown I was supposed to have worn lay in its various pieces across the chair. Too bad for Natalia it would go unworn today.

Possibly tomorrow.

Possibly for years.

I didn't know how quickly my need for Emrick would be sated.

Without breaking the kiss, I took hold of his hand and, finger by finger, pulled his glove free. He drew away from me, eyes dark with yearning, lips parted, breath racing, as he curled his fingers around the leather. For a moment I worried he'd regained his senses and was ready to leave before we went any further, abandoning me to the discomfort of unsatisfied lust. But then he tossed the glove onto the table and tugged off the other one to join the first.

With a shaking hand, he touched his bare fingers to my face. At the contact, another jolt spun through me, but again I remained right where I was, flesh, muscle, and bone singing, as far from Death as I could imagine being.

"You're so beautiful," he whispered. "My Katerina."

He caught my lips again and cradled my face in his palms. Every touch, every caress was an explosion of sensation, and I craved more. With eager hands, I crawled my fingers under his shirt and pulled it over his head, baring the wolf tattoo on his muscular chest in all its detail. His lips traced along my jaw and down my neck as he slid the shift over my shoulders and let it fall to the floor, then continued downwards, murmuring compliments on the softness of my skin, the perfection of my body. His deep voice vibrated against me, warming me to my core. When his mouth reached the apex between my thighs, my knees gave out, and he caught me before I fell, throwing me onto the bed before he continued tasting me, his tongue creating the same sparks through my blood as the rest of my contact with him. I buried my hands in his hair and held him close as my peak crept closer, but before it came, I pushed him away.

I needed more than the pleasure he promised. I needed *him*—his closeness, his presence. He heeded my wishes and kissed his way up my body. Lingering around my breasts as he untied his breeches and kicked them off.

When he settled between my legs, I cupped his cheek in my palm and took a moment to luxuriate in the weight of him. He rocked his hips against mine in slow, undulating waves, and I rose to meet him. His hard length pressed against my centre, teasing me with what was coming, but neither of us hurried.

Seventy-five years for me, hundreds for him, with all of eternity stretched out ahead of us. What was the need to rush?

I leaned up to kiss him, tasted my desire on his tongue, and sucked in a sharp breath as a surge of need passed through me.

What had I just been thinking about not needing to rush? What a fool I was.

I reached between us to take him in my hand and guide him where I wanted him, and he chuckled as he shifted.

On his next thrust, he was inside me, and my back arched

as I took him in, revelling in every tiny pleasure at the contact both inside and out. Never before had I experienced such exquisite sensations, every sweet feeling heightened, my skin, my blood, my bones on fire. I dug my nails into his back, pulling him closer, not satisfied until every part of him touched every part of me as he thrust against me, languidly at first but growing more demanding as our desire climbed.

"Kate," he whispered into the crook of my neck. *"Mîn êcnes."*

My eternity.

Those words, a simple statement of fact on one level but suggesting so much more, pushed me over the edge. I hung on to him as my peak rose to meet his, and I didn't let go until both of us were ready to come down together.

Epilogue

Katerina

Constantinople - 1453

ADRIAN, EMRICK, AND I stood outside the Hagia Sophia, the great church of Constantinople. For the last many nights, we'd held our ground against the undead rising from the tombs around the building, summoned by a group of witches looking to fight back the Turks threatening their shores.

Fire stretched from my back like wings as I drew lightning between my palms. With easy movements, I threw out sparks and fireballs flew, striking the crawling corpses and sending them back, burning, into their resting places. Adrian darted between them, tearing off their heads, moving so quickly all I made out was the carnage he wrought.

Emrick dotted the scene, escorting the souls and clearing away the bodies of the witches I took down.

We were ruthless. Relentless. A team to be feared, as many groups across many countries had come to learn.

For two hundred years, we'd travelled together, Adrian and I fighting anyone and anything that threatened the fragile balance between magical and mundane, Emrick and I losing ourselves in each other, the three of us finding a new balance.

Not a day went by that I didn't think about my family, not a decision made that I didn't weigh their values and beliefs against my own. Not once in three hundred years did I feel I'd paid my debt to their memory, but with every day that passed, I worked towards it.

Would continue to work towards it.

No matter what the future held, I knew my place in the world—and the world would be wise to watch out.

Thank You for Reading

Thank you so much for taking a chance on an independent author. We're living in a wonderful age where it's easy to upload a book to the internet, but that doesn't reflect the blood, sweat, and tears that go into making a book the best version it can be. It takes time, patience, perseverance, and to have the final result end up in a new reader's hands is the best reward. You are the reason we keep writing, so thank you.

If you enjoyed the read, please help support the author by leaving a review at the retailer where you purchased the book. Reviews make a world of difference for an author, helping us reach new audiences and bringing more people into the worlds you've spent time in.

For exclusive character content, announcements, promotions, and special offers, sign up for Krista's mailing list at https://www.kristawalshauthor.com/pages/about-the-author

Author's Note

While much research was done for the sake of accuracy, I know some errors might have crept in. There is also a degree of creative licence, because magic.

Acknowledgements

In my original original original draft of Kat's story, her past was interwoven with the present in every book. Although I decided to keep the current version predominantly in the present, I couldn't let Kat's entire history sit in obscurity, so of course there had to be a prequel.

A large chunk of what you've read was in the original version of book 2, repurposed and improved.

Thank you so much to everyone who read and gave feedback on this book. Kate Sparkes, the fantastic FAKAs, Christopher Barnes, my ARC readers and Street Team, my beta readers. You all made this possible!

Thank you to my husband, Chris Reddie, for walking me through my fight scenes—and to my daughter, for inadvertently helping me reenact them (ah, the joys of developing coordination).

Thank you to my Patrons, who have waited so patiently for this book and cheered me on the whole way.

And thank you to my readers for being so excited to get more of Kat & Emrick's past!

There's still more to come ^.^

About the Author

Known for witty, vivid characters, Krista Walsh never has more fun than getting them into trouble and taking her time getting them out.

When not writing, she can be found reading, gaming, or watching a film – anything to get lost in a good story.

She currently lives in Ottawa, Ontario with her husband, toddler, and epileptic blue heeler.

You can find her at www.kristawalshauthor.com or at the local Second Cup coffee shop... but only if you come bearing a Vanilla Bean Latte, half-sweet.

Other Works by Krista Walsh

Epic Fantasy
The Meratis Trilogy
The Cadis Trilogy
The Nayis Trilogy

Urban Fantasy
The Dark Descendants
The Ghostmaker Trilogy
The Immortal Sorceress Series